DON CAMILLO
AND HIS
FLOCK

Giovanni Guareschi
has also written
THE LITTLE WORLD OF DON CAMILLO

DON CAMILLO AND HIS

FLOCK by GIOVANNI GUARESCHI · Translated

by FRANCES FRENAYE

PELLEGRINI & CUDAHY : *New York*

CONTENTS

THE LITTLE WORLD

WHEN I WAS A YOUNG MAN I
worked as a reporter and went around all day on a bicycle
looking for news stories for the paper. One day I met a girl
and after that I spent so many hours thinking about how this
girl would feel if I became Emperor of Mexico, or maybe
died instead, that I had very little time left for anything else.
So at night I filled my allotted space with invented stories
which people liked very much because they were much more
true to life than true ones. Of course, there is nothing sur-

prising about this, because stories, like people, grow in a certain atmosphere. That's why geography is important.

The stories in this book take place somewhere in the valley of the Po river. I was born near the Po and it is the only respectable river in all Italy. To be respectable, a river must flow through a plain because water was created to stay horizontal and only when it is perfectly horizontal does it preserve its natural dignity. Niagara Falls is an embarrassing phenomenon, like a man who walks on his hands. Now the Po crosses the great plains of Northern Italy, and in a slice of land between the river and the mountains is a village, a Little World. People born near the Po river have heads as hard as pig iron, a highly developed sense of humor, and where politics is concerned they can get as excited as a man who has swallowed a mouse.

They are very attached to their slice of land and in spite of floods and fog, the fierce summer heat, and damp winter cold, they admit that, after all, God knew his business when He made the Little World.

This is all the geography you need in order to understand the village priest, Don Camillo, and his adversary, Peppone, the Communist mayor, and how it is that Christ watches the goings-on from a big cross in the village church and not infrequently speaks. And while I'm about it, I must say one thing that I always say when I begin to talk about the Little World. If there is a priest anywhere who feels offended by my treatment of Don Camillo, he is welcome to break the biggest candle available over my head. And if there is a Communist who feels offended by Peppone, he is welcome to break a hammer and sickle on my back. But if there is anyone who is offended by the conversations of Christ, I can't help it; for the one who speaks in this story is not Christ, but my Christ— that is, the voice of my conscience.

THE THIRTEENTH-CENTURY ANGEL

WHEN OLD BASSINI DIED they found written in his will: "I bequeath everything I have to the parish priest, Don Camillo, to be spent for gilding the angel on the church tower so that I can see it shining all the way from Heaven and recognize the place where I was born."

The angel was at the top of the bell tower and, from below, it did not appear to be very large. But when they had erected scaffolding and climbed up to see, they found it was almost the size of a man and would require quite an amount

:[3]:

of gold leaf to cover. An expert came from the city to examine the statue at close hand, and he came down a few minutes later in a state of great agitation.

"It's the Archangel Gabriel in beaten copper," he explained to Don Camillo. "A beautiful thing, straight from the thirteenth century."

Don Camillo looked at him and shook his head.

"Neither the church nor the tower is more than three hundred years old," he objected.

But the expert insisted that this didn't matter.

"I've been in business forty years, and I've gilded I can't tell you how many statues. If it isn't thirteenth century, I'll do the job for you free."

Don Camillo was a man who preferred to keep his feet firmly on the ground, but curiosity drove him to climb with the expert to the top of the tower and look the angel in the face. There he gaped in astonishment, for the angel was very beautiful indeed. He, too, was agitated when he came down, because he couldn't imagine how such a work of art had come to be on the bell tower of a humble country church. He dug into the parish archives, but found no account of it whatsoever. The next day the expert came back from the city with two gentlemen who went with him to the top of the tower, and they backed up his opinion that the statue was beyond a shadow of doubt thirteenth-century. They were two professors in the line of art, two important names, and Don Camillo could not find words with which to thank them.

"It's something quite wonderful!" he exclaimed. "A thirteenth-century angel on the tower of this poor little church! It's an honor for the whole village."

That afternoon a photographer came to take pictures of the statue from every possible angle. And the next morning a city newspaper carried an article, with three illustrations, which said it was a crime to leave such a treasure exposed to the

:[4]:

four winds, when it was part of the nation's cultural heritage and should be kept under shelter. Don Camillo's ears turned crimson as he read.

"If those city rascals think they're going to take our angel away, then they've got another guess coming," he said to the masons who were strengthening the scaffolding.

"That's right," said the masons. "It's ours, and nobody has a right to touch it."

Then some more important people arrived upon the scene, including representatives of the bishop, and as soon as they came down from looking at the angel they all told Don Camillo that it was a shame to leave it there, exposed to the weather.

"I'll buy him a raincoat," Don Camillo said in exasperation, and when they protested that this was an illogical thing to say he retorted with considerable logic: "In public squares all over the world statues have stood for centuries amid the raging elements and no one has dreamed of putting them under shelter. Why should we have to tuck our angel away? Just go tell the people of Milan that the Madonnina on that cathedral of theirs is falling to pieces and they ought to take it down and put it under cover. Don't you know that they'd give you a good, swift kick if you suggested anything of the kind?"

"The Madonnina of Milan is a very different matter," said one of the important visitors.

"But the kicks they give in Milan are very much like those we give here!" Don Camillo answered, and because the villagers crowding around him on the church square punctuated his last remark with a: "That's right!" no one pursued the subject further.

Some time later the city newspaper returned to the attack. To leave a beautiful thirteenth-century angel on the church tower of a valley village was a crime. Not because anyone

:[5]:

wanted to take the angel away, but because the village could make good money off tourists if only it were in a more accessible place. No art lover was going to travel so far, simply in order to stand in the square and gape up at a statue on top of a tower. They ought to bring the angel down into the church, have a cast made, and then an exact copy which they could gild and put in its place.

After people in the village had read that newspaper article, they began to mumble that there was something to it, and the local Communists, under the leadership of Mayor Peppone, couldn't very well pass up the opportunity to comment on "a certain reactionary who should have been born in the Middle Ages." As long as the angel stayed up on the tower, no one could appreciate its beauty. Down in the church it would be in plain sight, and there would be no loss to the tower if another angel were to replace it. Don Camillo's most prosperous parishioners talked it over with him, and eventually he admitted that he might have been in the wrong. When the angel was taken down the whole village gathered in the square, and it had to be left there for several days because people wanted to see and touch it. They came from miles around, for word had spread that the angel had miraculous powers. When the time came to make the cast, Don Camillo said stubbornly: "The angel's not to budge. Bring your tools and do the job here."

After the settlement of old Bassini's estate, it came out that he had left enough money to gild a dozen angels, and so there was plenty to spend on the bronze copy. The copy itself finally arrived from the city, all covered with gold, and everyone proclaimed it a masterpiece. People compared the measurements, inch by inch, and found that they tallied exactly.

"If the original were gilded too," they said, "no one could tell them apart."

However Don Camillo felt some scruples about his failure to carry out the terms of old Bassini's will.

"I'll have the original gilded, then," he said. "There's plenty of money."

But the people from the city intervened and said the original mustn't be tampered with. They presented a number of arguments, but Don Camillo had ideas of his own.

"It isn't a question of art," he insisted. "Bassini left me the money for the express purpose of gilding the angel on the tower. This is the angel he meant, and if I don't have it gilded, then I'm betraying his trust."

The new angel was hoisted to the top of the tower, and the experts proceeded to gild the old one. It was placed in a niche near the door, and everyone gaped at it in its shiny new dress.

The night before the unveiling of both statues, Don Camillo could not sleep. Finally he got up and went over to the church to look at the original angel.

"Thirteenth-century," he said to himself, "and this little church no more than three hundred years old! You existed four hundred years before the tower was built. How did you ever get up there?"

Don Camillo stared at the great wings of the Archangel Gabriel and ran his big hand over his perspiring face. How could a heavy copper angel like this one have flown up to the top of a tower? Now he stood in a niche, behind a glass door that could be opened and shut for protection. Impulsively Don Camillo took a key out of his pocket and opened the door. How could an angel that had lived on top of a tower stay shut up in a box? Surely he must be suffocating for want of air. And Don Camillo remembered the text of old Bassini's will: "I bequeath everything I have to the parish priest, Don Camillo, to be spent for gilding the angel on the church tower so that I can see it shining all the way from Heaven and recognize the place where I was born."

"And now he doesn't see his angel at all," Don Camillo reflected. "He sees a false angel in its place. That isn't what he wanted."

Don Camillo was very troubled and when that happened he went to kneel at the feet of Christ on the big cross over the altar.

"Lord," he said, "why did I cheat old Bassini? What made me give in to those rascals from the city?"

Christ did not answer, and so Don Camillo went back to the angel.

"For three hundred years you've watched over this valley and its people. Or perhaps, for seven hundred years. Who knows? For this church may have been built on the ruins of one much older. You have saved us from famine and plague and war. Who can say how many gales and bolts of lightning you have turned away? For three, or perhaps seven, hundred years, you have given the village's last farewell to the souls of the dead as they rose up into Heaven. Your wings have vibrated to the sound of the bells, whether they called men to rejoice or to mourn. Yes, centuries of joy and sorrow are in your wings. And now you are shut up in a gilded cage, where you will never see the sky or the sun again. Your place has been usurped by a false city angel, whose only memories are the swear words of unionized foundry workers. You took shape from an unknown thirteenth-century craftsman with faith to inspire his hammer, while the usurper was turned out by some monstrously unholy machine. How can a piti-less, mechanical creature like that protect us? What does he care for our land and its people?"

It was eleven o'clock at night and the village lay wrapped in silence and fog from the river when Don Camillo went out of the church and into the darkness.

Peppone was not in a good humor when he answered the knock at his door.

"I need you," said Don Camillo. "Put on your coat and follow me."

When they were inside the church the priest pointed to the captive angel.

"He protected your father and mother and their fathers and mothers before them. And he must watch over your son. That means going back to where he was before."

"Are you mad?" asked Peppone.

"Yes," said Don Camillo. "But I can't do it alone. I need the help of a madman like you."

The scaffolding was still up all around the tower. Don Camillo tucked his cassock into his trousers and began to climb, while Peppone followed him with a rope and pulley. Their madness lent them the strength of a dozen men. They lassooed the angel, detached it from its pedestal and lowered it to the ground. Then they carried it into the church, took the original angel out of the niche and put the false one in its place.

Five men had worked at hoisting the false angel up to the top of the tower, but now the two of them managed to do it alone. They were soaked with fog and perspiration and their hands were bleeding from the rope.

It was five o'clock in the morning. They lit a fire in the rectory and downed two or three bottles of wine in order to collect their thoughts. At this point they began to be afraid. Day was breaking, and they went to peer out the window. There was the angel, high above them, on top of the tower.

"It's impossible," said Peppone.

Suddenly he grew angry and turned upon Don Camillo.

"Why did you rope me into it?" he asked him. "What damned business is it of mine?"

"It isn't damned business at all," Don Camillo answered. "There are too many false angels loose in the world working against us already. We need true angels to protect us."

Peppone sneered.

"Silly religious propaganda!" he said, and went away without saying goodbye.

In front of his own door, something made him turn around and look up into the sky. There was the angel, shining in the first light of dawn.

"Hello there, Comrade!" Peppone mumbled serenely, taking off his cap to salute him.

Meanwhile Don Camillo knelt before the crucifix at the altar and said:

"Lord, I don't know how we did it!"

Christ did not answer, but he smiled, because He knew very well how.

LA ROCCA, THE TOWER

which was the center of the township and the seat of the town hall, was in a sad state of disrepair. When one day a squad of masons appeared upon the scene and began to throw up scaffolding around the tower, everybody said: "It's about time!"

It wasn't a question of looks, because in the Po river valley æsthetics matter very little, and a thing is beautiful when it is well made and serves its purpose. But everybody had occasion at one time or another to go to the town hall, and they didn't like the prospect of having a brick or a fragment of cornice fall upon their heads.

When the scaffolding was up, the masons swathed the façade with cloth so that no plaster would fall on the passers-by and then began the repairs. These went on for about a month, until one night everything was taken down, and the next morning the people of the village, along with a number of strangers who had come to the weekly market-day, found the tower completely restored. The masons knew their trade and had done a good job. Of course, they couldn't leave politics out of it and so they had hung up a big sign, near the top, which said: "*This public work was* NOT *financed by the Marshall Plan.*"

Don Camillo was among the crowd that had gathered in the square and when Peppone saw him he edged up behind his back and sprung on him the question: "Well, what have you got to say?"

Don Camillo did not even turn around. "A good job," he said. "Too bad that the looks of it should be ruined by that sign."

Peppone turned to a group of his henchmen, who just happened to be standing by.

"Did you hear? He says that the looks of the thing are ruined by the sign. Do you know, I very nearly agree!"

"Where artistic matters are concerned, the priest's word carries a lot of weight," Smilzo put in. "I think he's right."

They discussed it further, and finally Peppone said:

"Someone go tell them to take down that sign. That'll prove that we're not like certain people who claim to be infallible."

A couple of minutes later, someone loosened a rope, and the sign came down. And then appeared the real surprise: a magnificent new clock. For years and years the clock on the bell tower of the church had been the only public timepiece in the village, but now there was another on the town hall.

"You can't appreciate it fully in the daytime," Peppone exclaimed. "But the dial is transparent and lighted from inside, so that by night you can read the time from a mile away."

Just then there was a vague noise from the top of La Rocca and Peppone shouted:

"Silence!"

The square was full of people, but they all fell silent to listen to the new clock strike ten. Hardly had the echoes died away, when the clock on the church tower began to ring out the same hour.

"Wonderful," said Don Camillo to Peppone. "Only your clock is nearly two minutes fast."

Peppone shrugged his shoulders.

"One might just as well say that your clock is nearly two minutes slow."

Don Camillo did not lose his aplomb.

"One might just as well say so, but it's inadvisable. My clock is exact to the second, just as it has been for the last thirty or forty years, and there was no use squandering public funds for a new one on the town hall."

Peppone wanted to say any number of things, but there were so many he choked, and the veins of his neck stood out like ropes. Smilzo rushed into the breach, raising one finger.

"You're angry because you wanted to have a monopoly on time! But time doesn't belong exclusively to the clergy! It belongs to the people!"

The new clock struck a quarter past the hour, and once more the square was silent. First one and then two minutes went by.

"It's more inaccurate than before!" exclaimed Don Camillo. "Now it's a full two minutes fast."

People took big silver watches out of their vest pockets

:[13]:

and began to argue. It was all very strange, because before this none of them had ever cared about minutes at all. Minutes and seconds are strictly city preoccupations. In the city people hurry, hurry so as not to waste a single minute, and fail to realize that they are throwing a lifetime away.

When the town hall clock struck half-past ten, and the bell tower followed, two minutes later, there were two schools of opinion. The conflict was not a violent one, because it remained within the circumference of the opposing parties' vest pockets. But Smilzo had warmed up to all the implications, and shouted:

"On the day when the La Rocca clock strikes the hour of the people's revolution, some people are going to find out that they're not two minutes but two centuries behind!"

Smilzo always talked that way, but this time he made the mistake of shaking a threatening finger under Don Camillo's nose. And Don Camillo made an unequivocal answer. He stretched out his hand, pulled Smilzo's cap down over his eyes and then did the classical turn of the screw, leaving the visor at the back of his neck. Peppone stepped forward.

"What would you say if anyone played that trick on you?" he asked through his teeth.

"Try and see!" said Don Camillo. "No one's ever tried so far!"

Twenty hands dragged Peppone back.

"Don't do anything rash," they said. "The mayor mustn't get into trouble."

The gang of Reds closed in on Don Camillo and began to shout. Don Camillo had an urge to create some fresh air about him and a bench was the first fan that came into his hand. With his steam up and a bench in his grasp, Don Camillo was a cyclone. In a second there was an empty space around him, but since the square was packed with people and market-stands, an empty space at one point meant increased density at some other. A chicken cage was trampled, a horse reared, and there was a chorus of shouts, moos and whinnies. The Red gang was routed, but Peppone, who was squashed into the entrance of the town hall by people who didn't want him to get in trouble, managed to seize a bench in his turn. And Peppone, too, when his motor was running at high speed, and he had a bench in his grasp, was a tornado that knew neither friend nor foe. The crowd stepped back, while Peppone slowly and fatefully advanced toward Don Camillo, who stood his ground, bench in hand. The crowd had retreated to the periphery of the square, and only Smilzo kept his head and threw himself in Peppone's way.

"Forget it, Chief! Don't behave like a donkey!"

But Peppone implacably advanced toward the center of the square, and Smilzo had to back up as he delivered his warning. Suddenly he found himself between the two benches, but he stood firm and awaited the shock of the earthquake. The crowd was silent. The most desperate of the Reds had grouped themselves behind Peppone, and Don Camillo was backed up by a group of old peasants, who had a nostalgic longing for the blackjack, and now shook their stout cherry sticks at their opponents. There seemed to be a tacit agreement between both sides. As soon as Peppone and Don Camillo let go with their benches, there would be a free-for-all fight. There was a moment of deathly silence while the two protagonists brandished their weapons, and then something extraordinary happened. The old clock and the new both started to strike eleven, and their strokes were in perfect synchronization.

The benches fell, and the empty middle of the square filled up with people. As if they were coming out of a dream, Don Camillo and Peppone found themselves in a busy marketplace, where vendors were crying their wares. Peppone went off to the town hall and Don Camillo to the rectory.

Smilzo was left alone in the middle of the square, trying to figure out what had happened. Finally he gave up trying to understand, and since all the Reds had melted away he went over to a near-by stand and drank a coca-cola.

RHADAMES

RHADAMES WAS THE SON
of Badile, the locksmith, whose real name was Hernani
Gniffa. Obviously an operatic family. Badile had a good
ear, and when he had tucked away a bottle or two of wine
he sang with a powerful voice that was a pleasure to hear.
When Badile's son, Rhadames, was six years old, his father
brought him to Don Camillo and asked to have him taken
into the choir. Don Camillo tested the boy's voice and then
said:

"The only thing I can do is set him to blowing the organ

bellows." For Rhadames had a voice as hard and cutting as a splinter of stone.

"He's my son," said Badile, "so he must have a voice. It's still tight, that's all. All it needs is loosening up."

To say no would have meant giving Badile the worst disappointment of his life, so the priest sighed and said, "I'll do my best."

Don Camillo did everything he could, but after two years, Rhadames' voice was worse than ever. Besides being even harsher than before, it stuck in his throat. Rhadames had a magnificent chest, and to hear a miserable squeak come out of it was really infuriating. One day Don Camillo lost patience, got up from the organ and gave Rhadames a kick that landed him against the wall. Where singing is concerned, a kick may be more effective than three years' study of harmony: Rhadames went back to the choir and came out with a voice that seemed to emerge straight from La Scala. When people heard him, they said that it would be a crime for him to discontinue his studies.

This is the way they are in a village. If a fellow is disagreeable and unattractive they'll let him die of starvation. But if they take a liking to a fellow, they'll put together the money to get him singing lessons. In this case, they collected enough to send Rhadames to the city. Not to live like a gentleman—that couldn't be expected—but with his singing lessons paid for. And for the rest, Rhadames had to earn his board and keep by sawing wood, delivering parcels, and so on. Every now and then Badile went to see him and brought back the news: "He's not doing too badly. He's making progress."

Then the war came along, and Rhadames was lost from sight. One day when it was all over he turned up in the village. Peppone was mayor, and when Don Camillo told him that Rhadames' musical education must go on, he found the money to send him back to the city. A year or two later, Rhadames turned up again.

"They're letting me sing in *Aïda*," he said.

Things were tense in the village for political reasons, and violence was in the air, but on account of this news hostilities were suspended. Peppone held a meeting at the town hall, and Don Camillo attended it. The first question that came up was how to raise funds.

"The honor of the village is at stake," Peppone explained. "Rhadames mustn't cut a poor figure before those big shots in the city."

And the committee agreed.

"If anyone can get money out of those that have it," said Peppone, "I can guarantee the support of the common people."

Don Camillo understood that this was a gentle hint, and answered. "Somebody will do it."

Then Rhadames gave a detailed account of his needs, which was found quite satisfactory.

"Here there's no question of corruption or special favors," Peppone said proudly. "This is definitely a proletarian victory."

Don Camillo turned to Rhadames.

"What is your stage name?" he asked him.

"His stage name?" shouted Peppone. "His own, of course! Do you want him to assume yours?"

Don Camillo did not lose his temper.

"Rhadames Gniffa isn't the kind of name you can put on an opera program. It's a most unfortunate name, because it's bound to make people laugh."

Then Rhadames' father came into the discussion.

"My name is Hernani Gniffa, and I've borne it for sixty-five years without anyone's laughing!"

"That's all very well, but you're a locksmith, not a tenor!"

Don Camillo answered. "Around here nobody cares, but in the theatrical world, it's a different matter. There you need a name that sounds well and is sure to be popular."

"How ridiculous!" exclaimed Peppone. "Middle-class stupidity!"

Don Camillo looked at him hard.

"If Giuseppe Verdi had been called Rhadames Gniffa, do you think he would have won fame as a composer?"

Peppone stopped to think, and Don Camillo gave him another example. "If Joseph Stalin had happened to be called Euripedes Bergnocioni, would he have left the same mark on history?"

"The very idea!" stammered Peppone. "Think of Stalin under the name of Bergnocioni! Impossible!"

The committee sat until late at night, and finally made a unanimous choice of the name Franco Santalba.

"It's a queer world!" they all said.

Rhadames shrugged his shoulders. "Whatever you decide is all right with me," he said.

The great day came at last, and the committee met in the village square to read the announcement of the opera in the newspaper that had just arrived from the city. Rhadames' photograph was there, and under it the caption: "Franco Santalba, tenor." They couldn't resist going to hear him.

"There's room in the truck for all of us," said Peppone. "And we'd better make an early start in order to get seats. We'll meet here in the square at four o'clock."

"Somebody must tell the priest," one of the men observed. "He won't be able to come, but he ought to know about it."

"Priests don't interest me," said Peppone.

But they went to the rectory in a body.

"I can't go, you know that," Don Camillo said sadly. "It

wouldn't do for a priest to go to the opera, especially on the opening night. You'll have to tell me all about it."

When the committee had gone, Don Camillo went to confide his sorrow to Christ on the altar.

"I'm distressed that I can't go," he said with a sigh. "Rhadames is almost like a son to us all. But of course duty is duty. My place is here, and not amid the worldly frivolities of a theatre . . ."

"Quite right, Don Camillo. One of those small sacrifices that you must accept cheerfully."

"Yes, of course from a general or absolute point of view, it's a small sacrifice," said Don Camillo. "But to the person concerned, it's a large one. Of course, the greater the sacrifice it is, the more cheerfully it should be accepted. Complaints take all the value of a sacrifice away. In fact, if a sacrifice brings out a complaint, it doesn't count as a sacrifice at all."

"Naturally," Christ answered.

Don Camillo paced up and down the empty church.

"I developed the boy's voice," he explained, stopping in front of the altar. "He came not much higher than my knees, and he couldn't sing; he squeaked like a rusty chain. And now he's singing in *Aïda*. Rhadames in *Aïda!* And I can't hear him. Surely, that's a tremendous sacrifice. But I'm bearing up very cheerfully."

"Certainly you are," whispered Christ with a smile.

Peppone and his gang sat in the front row of the gallery with their heads whirling. To gain admission to the gallery, it's not sufficient to pay for a ticket; one has to fight for a seat as well. And when *Aïda* is on the boards the gallery is a madhouse. That evening, however, a burly man made his way through the crowd at the last minute and came in just behind Peppone. He was wearing a green coat, and Peppone seemed to know him, because he squeezed over on the bench and made a place for him.

"If Rhadames loses his nerve, he's out of luck," Peppone mumbled. "This is a merciless crowd."

"Here's hoping," said the burly man in the green coat.

"If they hiss him, I'll kill somebody," said Peppone excitedly, and the man in the green coat motioned to him to keep his head.

But they didn't whistle; they were kind enough simply to snicker. Toward the end of the first act, things got worse and worse. Rhadames was scared pink and sang way off key. The gallery howled, vigorously enough to make the curtain tremble. Peppone clenched his teeth, and his stalwarts were ready to sow murder around them. But the burly man took Peppone by the collar and dragged him outside. They walked up and down in the fresh air, and when they heard a howl, they knew that Rhadames had hit still another false note. Then the triumphal march caused the audience to calm down. Shortly before the third act, the burly man said to Peppone: "Let's go."

The attendants didn't want to admit them behind the scenes. But before two strapping men with the combined strength of an armored division, there was nothing to do. They found Rhadames waiting in terror to be howled off the stage for the third and last time. When he saw the two men, his jaw fell open. The man in the green coat went around behind him and gave him a kick powerful enough to launch a Caruso.

Rhadames practically sailed through the air onto the stage, but he was completely transformed when he got there. When he sang the great aria *"Io son disonorato!"* the theatre almost broke down under the applause.

"You've got to know a singer down to the bottom," the burly man said triumphantly to the hysterical Peppone.

"Yes, Don . . ." Peppone started to reply, but at one look from the burly man he broke his sentence off in the middle.

:[22]:

THE STUFF FROM AMERICA

THE PARTY DELEGATE
was one of those gloomy, tight-lipped characters who seem
to have been made just for wearing a red scarf around the
neck and a Tommy gun slung over one shoulder. The reason
for his visit to the village was to *galvanize* and *activate* the
local section of the Party. He made endless speeches to the
cell leaders, for when these gloomy, tight-lipped fellows start
talking politics they are as long-winded as the late Adolf
Hitler. He stayed three whole days, and on the morning of the

third day, when he had finished laying down the latest Party line, he said to Peppone:

"Saturday you're to call a meeting of the village council and announce that you're resigning from the post of mayor."

"Have I done so badly?" stammered Peppone.

"No, Comrade; you've done so well that you're to be promoted. You're to run for Parliament on the People's Front ticket."

"Me run for Parliament?"

"Yes, that's what I said."

"But I haven't any education . . ."

"You know how to obey, Comrade, don't you? All a deputy to Parliament needs to know is how to obey Party orders. And you're sure to attract votes. You're known all over the province for the way you hustle around and get things done."

Peppone threw out his arms.

"But what about my own village?"

"Do you care more for the community than for Communism?"

Peppone bowed his head.

"Of course you'll have to make some campaign speeches. But we'll send you those, don't worry. You can just learn them by heart."

While the delegate was giving him further instructions as to how to conduct his campaign, Smilzo burst breathlessly into the room.

"The stuff from America is here!" he shouted. "I mean the foodstuff. There are posters up to announce that the needy can call at the rectory for relief parcels. Spaghetti, canned milk, preserves, butter and sugar. The posters have created quite a sensation."

"What's the exact wording of the announcement?" the delegate asked him.

*"The fatherly heart of His Holiness . . . etc. . . . etc.
. . . parcels which all the needy are entitled to receive upon
application to the parish priest, Don Camillo . . . etc. . . .
etc. . . ."*

"*All* the needy, did you say?"

"Yes, all of them, without distinction."

Peppone clenched his fists.

"I knew that devil was cooking up something of the sort,"
he said. "They speculate on human misery, the filthy cowards.
We'll have to do something about it."

"Yes, Comrade, do something!" the delegate ordered.
"Call a meeting of the cell leaders."

After the cell leaders had hastened to answer the call, Peppone informed them of the latest reactionary manoeuver.

"Within half an hour the comrades must be told that if
one of them accepts so much as a safety-pin I'll strangle him
for it. Smilzo, you stand guard in front of the rectory. Keep
your eyes peeled every minute and take down the names of all
those who go to pick up parcels."

"Well spoken," the delegate said approvingly. "A case
like this requires decisive action."

All day long there was a line in front of the rectory. The
priest was jubilant, because the parcels were plentiful and
well filled and people were happy to get them.

"Tell me if the so-called People's Party gives you anything
better," he said, laughing.

"They give nothing but big talk," everyone answered.

Some of the Reds were needy enough, but they didn't show
up. This was the only fly in the priest's ointment, because he
had prepared a special homily for their benefit. "You haven't
any right to this, since you have Stalin to look after you. But
take a parcel just the same, Comrade, and here's luck to you!"

When none of the Reds put in an appearance and the priest was told that Smilzo was standing behind a bush, taking down the name of everyone who went away with a parcel, he realized that he would have to keep his homily to himself. By six o'clock in the evening all the "regular" needy had been taken care of and there were left only the parcels meant for "special cases." Don Camillo went into the church to talk to Christ.

"See here, Lord, what do You think of that?"

"I see, Don Camillo, and I must admit I find it touching. Those people are just as poor as the rest, but they're putting Party loyalty above their hunger. And so Don Camillo has lost a chance to deliver some sarcastic remarks at their expense."

Don Camillo lowered his head.

"Christian charity doesn't mean giving the crumbs from your table to the poor; it means dividing with them something that you need yourself. When Saint Martin divided his cloak with a beggar, that was Christian charity. And even when you share your last crust of bread with a beggar, you mustn't act as if you were throwing a bone to a dog. You must give humbly and thank him for allowing you to have a part in his hunger. Today you simply played the part of an altruist and the crumbs you distributed were from someone else's table, not your own. You had no merit. And instead of being humble, you had poison in your heart."

Don Camillo shook his head. "Lord," he whispered, "just send some of those poor Reds to me. I won't say a thing. I don't think I'd really have said anything before, either. You'd have shown me the light before I could say it."

Then he went back to the rectory and waited. After an hour had gone by, he closed the door and the front window. But after another hour he heard a knock at the door. The priest ran to open it, and there was Straziami, one of Peppone's most loyal followers, looking just as frowning and glum as ever.

He stood silently at the entrance for a moment and then said:

"I don't think any the better of you and your friends, and I intend to vote as I please. So don't say I misled you."

The priest barely nodded. Then he took one of the remaining parcels out of the cupboard and handed it to him. Straziami took it and tucked it away under his coat.

"Tell me the truth, Father," he said ironically. "You might very well make a good joke out of the sight of Comrade Straziami sneaking in for a relief parcel from America."

"Go out through the garden," was all the priest said in reply, and he lit the butt of his cigar.

Peppone and the Party delegate were having supper when Smilzo came to report.

"It's quarter past eight, and the priest has gone to bed."

"Is everything in good order?" asked Peppone.

"On the whole, yes," Smilzo said with some hesitation.

"Speak up, Comrade," said the delegate harshly. "Tell us the entire story."

"Well, all day long there was just the usual crowd, and I got all the names. Then just a quarter of an hour ago, a latecomer went into the rectory and it was too dark for me to see who he was."

Peppone clenched his fists.

"Out with it, Smilzo! Who was he?"

"It looked like one of our people to me . . ."

"Which one?"

"It looked like Straziami. But I can't swear to it."

They finished their supper in silence, and then the delegate stood up. "Let's investigate," he said. "Such things mustn't be allowed to ride too long."

Straziami's little boy was pale and thin, with big eyes, and hair that tumbled over his forehead. Small for his age, he looked a lot and said little. Now he sat at the kitchen table and stared with wide-open eyes at his father, who was glumly prying open a jar of fruit.

"That's for dessert," said his mother. "First have your spaghetti and canned milk."

She brought the bowl to the table and stirred its steaming contents, while Straziami went to sit down by the wall, between the fireplace and the cupboard. From this vantage point he gazed wonderingly at his son, whose eyes wandered in bewilderment from his mother's hands to the jar of fruit and then to the can of milk on the table.

"Aren't you coming to supper?" the woman said to Straziami.

"I don't want anything to eat," he mumbled.

She sat down across from the boy and was just about to fill his plate with spaghetti when Peppone and the Party delegate threw open the door. The delegate looked at the spaghetti and examined the labels on the milk and the jar of fruit.

"Where did you get this stuff?" he said harshly to Straziami, who had risen hesitatingly to his feet.

He waited in vain for an answer. Then he calmly gathered the four corners of the tablecloth into his hand, picked it up and threw it out the window. The little boy trembled, holding both hands in front of his mouth and staring at the delegate with terror. The woman had taken refuge against the wall and Straziami stood in the middle of the room with his arms hanging at his sides, as if he had been turned into stone. The delegate closed the window, walked over to Straziami and struck him across the face. A thread of blood trickled out of one corner of Straziami's mouth, but he did not move. The delegate went to the door and then turned around to say:

"That's Communism for you, Comrade. And if you don't like it, you can leave it."

His voice aroused Peppone, who had been gaping from one corner of the room as if the whole thing were a dream. They walked away in silence through the dark countryside, and Peppone could hardly wait to get home. In front of the inn the delegate held out his hand.

"I'm leaving at five o'clock tomorrow morning," he said. "You've got everything straight, haven't you? Saturday you resign and put Brusco in your place. You're to make your first speech at Castellino and tomorrow you'll receive the main body of the text. You can insert references to local conditions in the blank spaces. Goodnight, Comrade."

"Goodnight."

Peppone went straight to Smilzo's.

"I'll beat him up," he said to himself, but when he reached the door he hesitated and retraced his steps. He found himself in front of the rectory, but there he did not linger either.

"That's Communism for you, Comrade. And if you don't like it, you can leave it." The delegate's words were imprinted in his mind. At home he found his own son still awake in his crib, smiling and holding out his arms.

"Go to sleep," Peppone said brusquely. He spoke in so harsh and threatening a voice that no one, not even he himself, could have suspected that he was thinking of the wide-open eyes of Straziami's son.

In the room at the inn the Party delegate's mind was quite empty. He was fast asleep, satisfied with both himself and his Communism. But there was still a frown on his face, because Communists are on duty even when they are sleeping.

A MATTER OF CONSCIENCE

FOR SOME TIME PEPPONE
had been bringing the hammer down on the anvil, but no
matter how accursedly hard he struck it, he could not get
a certain tormenting thought out of his mind.

"The fool!" he mumbled to himself. "He's going to make a
mess!"

Just then he raised his eyes and saw the fool standing before him.

"You scared my boy," Straziami said gloomily. "He was restless all night long, and now he's in bed with fever."

"It's your own fault," said Peppone, hammering away, with his eyes on his work.

"Is it my fault that I'm poor?"

"You had orders, and Party orders have to be obeyed without discussion."

"Hungry children come before the Party."

"No, the Party comes before everything."

Straziami took something out of his pocket and laid it on the anvil.

"I'm turning in my card. It doesn't stand for Party membership anymore; it just means that I'm under special surveillance."

"Straziami, I don't like your way of talking."

"I'll talk as I choose. I won my freedom at the risk of my own skin, and I'm not going to give it up so lightly."

Peppone put down the hammer and wiped his forehead with the back of one hand. Straziami was one of the old guard; they had fought side by side, sharing the same hunger and hope and despair.

"You're betraying the cause," said Peppone.

"Isn't the cause freedom? If I give up my freedom, then I'm betraying the cause."

"We'll have to throw you out, you know. You're not allowed to resign. If you turn in your card, you'll be thrown out."

"I know it. And anyone that cheats too much is thrown out three months before he does it. To think that we have the nerve to call other people hypocrites! So long, Peppone. I'm sorry that you'll have to consider me your enemy when I'll still look on you as a friend."

Peppone watched Straziami walk away. Then he took hold

of himself, threw the hammer into the corner with a loud curse, and went to sit in the garden back of the workshop. He couldn't get used to the idea that Straziami had to be thrown out of the Party. Finally he jumped to his feet.

"It's all the fault of that damned priest," he decided. "Here's where I get him."

The "damned priest" was in the rectory, leafing through some old papers, when Peppone came in.

"I hope you're happy!" Peppone said angrily. "At last you've managed to hurt one of our people."

Don Camillo shot him a curious glance.

"Is the election affecting your mind?" he asked.

"Proud of yourself, aren't you? Just to have ruined a fellow's reputation, when this social system of yours has given him nothing but trouble."

"Comrade Mayor, I still don't understand."

"You'll understand well enough when I tell you that it's all your fault if Straziami is thrown out of the Party. You took advantage of the fact that he's so poor to lure him into accepting one of your filthy food parcels from America. Our Party delegate got wind of it and caught him at his own house, redhanded. He threw the food out the window and struck him across the face."

It was clear that Peppone was highly excited.

"Calm yourself, Peppone," said the priest.

"Calm yourself, my eye! If you'd seen Straziami's boy when the food was practically taken off his plate and he watched his father being struck, you wouldn't be calm. That is, not if you had any feelings."

Don Camillo turned pale and got up. He asked Peppone to tell him again exactly what the Party delegate had done. Then Don Camillo shook an accusing finger in Peppone's face.

"You swindler!" he exclaimed.

"Swindler yourself, for trying to take advantage of poor people's hunger and get them to vote for you!"

Don Camillo picked up an iron poker standing up in one corner of the fireplace.

"If you open your mouth again, I'll slaughter you!" he shouted. "I haven't speculated on anybody's starvation. I have food parcels to distribute and I haven't denied them to anyone. I'm interested in poor people's hunger, not their votes. You're the swindler! Because you have nothing to give away except printed papers full of lies, you won't let anyone have anything else. When somebody gives people things they need you accuse him of trying to buy votes, and if one of your followers accepts, you brand him as a traitor to the people. You're the traitor, I say, because you take away what someone else has given. So I was playing politics, was I? Making propaganda? Straziami's boy and the children of your other poor comrades who haven't the courage to come for food parcels don't know that they come from America. These children don't even know that there is such a place. All they know is that you're cheating them of the food they need. If a man sees that his children are hungry you'd say that he's entitled to steal a crust of bread for them to eat, but you wouldn't let him take it from America. And all because the prestige of Russia might suffer! But tell me, what does Straziami's boy know about America and Russia? He was just about to tuck away the first square meal he's seen for some time when you snatched it out of his mouth. I say that you're the swindler."

"I didn't say or do a thing."

"You let another man do it. And then you stood by while he did something even worse, while he struck a father in the presence of his child. A child has complete confidence in his father; he thinks of him as all-powerful and untouchable. And you let that double-faced deputy destroy the only treasure of

Straziami's unfortunate boy. How would you like it if I were to come to your house this evening and beat you up in front of your son?"

Peppone shrugged his shoulders. "You may as well get it out of your system," he said.

"I will!" shouted Don Camillo, livid with rage. "I'll get it out of my system, all right." He grasped both ends of the poker, clenched his teeth and with a roar like a lion's bent it double.

"I can throw a noose around you and your friend Stalin as well," he shouted. "And after I've got you in it, I can pull it tight, too."

Peppone watched him with considerable concern and made no comment. Then Don Camillo opened the cupboard and took out of it a parcel which he handed to Peppone.

"If you're not a complete idiot, take this to him. It doesn't come from America, or England, or even Portugal, for that matter. It's a gift of Divine Providence, which doesn't need anybody's vote to rule over the universe. If you want to, you can send for the rest of the parcels and distribute them yourself."

"All right. I'll send Smilzo with the truck," muttered Peppone, hiding the parcel under his coat. When he reached the door he turned around, laid the parcel on a chair, picked up the bent poker and tried to straighten it out.

"If you can do it, I'll vote for the 'People's Front'," leered Don Camillo.

Peppone's effort made him red as a tomato. The bar would not return to its original shape, and he threw it down on the floor.

"We don't need your vote to win," he said, picking up the parcel and going out the door.

Straziami was sitting in front of the fire, reading the paper, with his little boy crouching beside him. Peppone walked in, put the parcel on the table and untied it.

"This is for you," he said to the boy, "straight from the Almighty." Then he handed something to Straziami: "And here's something that belongs to you," he added. "You left it on my anvil."

Straziami took his Party membership card and put it into his wallet.

"Is that from the Almighty too?" he asked.

"The Almighty sends us everything," muttered Peppone, "the good along with the bad. You can't ever tell who's going to get what. This time we're lucky."

The little boy had jumped to his feet and was admiring the profusion of good things spilled out on the table.

"Don't worry; no one's going to take it away from you," Peppone said reassuringly.

Smilzo came with the truck in the afternoon.

"The chief sent me to pick up some stuff," he said to Don Camillo, who pointed out the parcels waiting stacked up for him in the hall.

When Smilzo came to pick up the last lot of them, Don Camillo followed him as he staggered under his load out the door and gave him a kick so hearty that both Smilzo and half of his parcels landed in the truck.

"Make a note of this along with the list of names you gave to the Party delegate," Don Camillo explained.

"We'll settle with you on election day," said Smilzo, extricating himself from the confusion. "Your name is at the head of another list of ours."

"Anything more I can do for you?"

"No. But I still don't get it. I've had the same treatment

:[35]:

from Peppone and Straziami already. And all because I carried out an order."

"Wrong orders shouldn't be carried out," Don Camillo warned him.

"Right. But how can one know ahead of time that they're wrong?" asked Smilzo with a sigh.

D ON CAMILLO HAD SOME-
thing on his mind that would give him no peace. It all began
the day he met the "live corpse," a young man who had supposedly died while in the mountains with Peppone and his
men during the Resistance. Don Camillo himself had officiated
at the funeral and followed the coffin to the cemetery. Then
one day after the war was over, Don Camillo caught a glimpse
of this same young man in the city who was far from being
dead as a mutton.

But it wasn't the walking corpse that bothered Don Camillo because he discovered that the coffin had contained not a dead body but a collection of loot seized from the Germans. He also knew that Peppone and his men had used the loot to finance the building of their People's Palace, and just because he had run across this useful bit of information as well as the walking corpse he had been able to persuade Peppone and his followers to make a modest contribution to the building of a Recreation Center for the children of the village. And there the matter rested. The People's Palace was built and the Recreation Center had a swing which was the delight of the children —especially Peppone's son who played on it by the hour, chirping joyfully like a fledgling. But the question bothering Don Camillo was how Peppone's men had managed to smuggle the coffin containing the loot out of the cemetery in the first place without attracting attention.

The cemetery served the whole township and was therefore fairly large. It lay outside the village and was built on the conventional plan, that is, enclosed by four walls, one of which had an entrance gate. These walls were bare and plain on the outside while on the inside they formed an arcade over rows of tombs.

In order to solve the mystery, Don Camillo took upon himself the role of Nat Pinkerton and went to examine the cemetery. Halfway down the left-hand arcade, in the second row, he found the famous niche, bearing a marble tablet on which was carved the fake name of the fake corpse. He turned his back on the niche and proceeded to walk straight through the grassy plot, studded with crosses, until he came to the central aisle. There he wheeled around in the direction of the gate and counted the number of steps it took him to reach it. The next day he walked inconspicuously along the path running parallel to the outside of the left wall, once more counting his steps, and when he had counted enough of them he stopped to light the butt of a cigar. The wall was overgrown with vines, but an attentive eye could see that about three feet above the ground, at a point corresponding to the niche the priest had inspected the day before, there was a section of plaster of a lighter color than the rest. And Don Camillo's eye was an attentive one.

"This is the way the treasure came out, and where one object came out another can go in. The thing about holes is that they allow two-way traffic."

He continued his walk, stopping in front of the police station to chat with the sergeant. That night the police quietly made a hole in the cemetery wall, at the point where Don Camillo had noticed the different shade of plaster, and out of the niche they took one machine-gun, thirty-eight Tommy guns, and twenty-three pistols, all of them so shiny and carefully oiled that they would have tempted any hothead to launch the "second phase of the revolution" then and there. The news created quite a stir and even got into the big-city papers, but no one came to claim the guns. At that point the story had seemed to fizzle out, because Don Camillo took care to make no reference to anything that had happened.

"When God gives you an inch, don't take a mile," he said to the police sergeant, when the latter tried to get something more out of him. "You ought to be glad you've got the guns."

"I can't be so easily satisfied. Now that I've found them I feel I must find the dead man whose place they were taking."

"I understand, but I wouldn't worry about him, Sergeant," Don Camillo advised him. "The guns are more important. After all, they can shoot, and that's more than a dead man can do."

Peppone, of course, had no comment to make, but he was about as easy in his mind as a man who has swallowed a mouse.

"*He* must have done it," he shouted to Brusco. "No one

would dig a hole in a tomb unless he was sure there was no-body in it. But I'll make him pay."

He, of course, was Don Camillo, who continued to be ex-tremely discreet. All he did was to plaster the walls of the "People's Palace" and Peppone's workshop with signs read-ing:

FOUND

Near the local cemetery, the corpse of the "second phase of the Revolution." Claimants apply to the police.

Five days later the village woke up to find itself covered with big yellow posters bearing the following notice:

LOST

Six hundred pounds of dried foods and canned groceries consigned by the Regional Relief Committee to the priest, Don Camillo, for distribution to the needy. If Don Camillo finds these goods, will he please turn them over to their rightful owners.

Signed: *The Village Needy.*
Death to all thieves!

Don Camillo rushed indignantly to the police station.

"I'll report them!" he shouted. "I'll report and accuse them, every one! This is an outrage!"

"Who's to be accused?" asked the sergeant. "The notice is signed 'the village needy'."

" 'Needy' indeed! The village riffraff! Peppone and his gang are trying to put this over."

"That may be. But we have only your word for it. Go ahead and file your complaint, and then we'll investigate."

Don Camillo started to go home, but in the square he pulled down the first poster that caught his eye and tore it into small pieces.

"Go on! Tear it up!" a man shouted to him from a bicycle. "But truth will out!"

And a ragged and dishevelled woman added her cries to his:

"Look at the priest's bulk!" she jeered. "He's grown fat on the food he stole from the poor!"

Don Camillo went his way, and a little farther on he met Filotti.

"Do you see what I see, Signor Filotti?" he asked him.

"Yes, I see," answered Filotti calmly. "But you mustn't let it bother you. I'm sure you can clear yourself. If I were you, I'd put up a poster reproducing your receipts for the groceries and the list of the persons to whom you distributed them."

"What receipts? What groceries?"

"The groceries from the Regional Relief Committee."

"But I didn't receive anything!" Don Camillo shouted. "And I didn't know such a committee existed!"

"Good Heavens! Is that possible?"

"It's more than possible; it's the literal truth! I never received a single thing!"

"How's that? It's unbelievable that anyone should make up a story of the kind. But if you say so, it must be true . . ."

Farther along the way Don Camillo ran into Signor Borghetti, who was reading the poster through spectacles perched on the end of his nose.

"This is a wicked world, Don Camillo," he said, shaking his head.

Old Barchini, the printer, was standing at the door of his shop.

"I didn't print it," he explained. "If they'd given me the job, I'd have told you about it. What about these groceries, Don Camillo? Are these the goods we were supposed to get from the Bishop?"

Just then Peppone's truck went by with Smilzo at the wheel.

"Here's a good appetite to you!" he called out, and everyone laughed.

Don Camillo ate no lunch. At three o'clock he was still lying on his bed and staring up at the beams of the ceiling. At four o'clock an infernal clamor rose from the church square and he looked out to see what was happening. There was an enormous crowd below, and as might have been expected, the front ranks were filled by women. Don Camillo found most of their faces unfamiliar, and he thought back to Smilzo and the truck.

"They've picked up roughnecks from all the surrounding villages," he said to himself. "They know how to organize, I'll grant them that."

"We want our groceries!" the women and children shouted. "Down with the exploiters of the people!"

"I've nothing to give you," shouted back Don Camillo from the window. "Because no one gave anything to me. It's a miserable lie!"

"We want to see for ourselves," a woman shouted, shaking her fists at him. "If you have nothing to hide, let us see!"

The crowd surged against the rectory door, and Don Camillo withdrew from the window and took his shotgun down from the wall. Then he laid it on the bed and went to look out again. The police sergeant and six of his men were standing guard at the rectory door. But the crowd seemed to have gone wild and was still clamoring to get in. At this point Peppone stepped forward.

"Quiet," he shouted. "I have something to say."

The crowd kept silence, and Peppone looked up at the window.

"Don Camillo," said Peppone, "I am speaking as mayor. This is no time to argue about whether what the poster says is false or true. These people feel that they have been cheated and they are justified in protesting. In order to avoid bloodshed, you must allow a committee to inspect the rectory. The committee will include myself and the village council and also the police sergeant with his men."

"Bravo!" shouted the crowd.

Don Camillo shook his head.

"There's nothing to see," he said. "This is my house, and I won't have it invaded. The poster was a lie from beginning to end; I'll swear to that on the Gospel."

"Swear to it on the cupboard where you've stowed away six hundred pounds of our groceries!" the crowd shouted. "You're not going to get away with it so easily."

Don Camillo shrugged his shoulders and stepped back. The crowd threw itself against the policemen and threatened to engulf them. But the sergeant kept his presence of mind and fired a shot into the air. The crowd retreated far enough for the police to pull themselves together and take a new position of defense.

"Stay where you are, or I'll have to use force of arms!" shouted the sergeant.

The crowd hesitated, then moved slowly but resolutely forward. The policemen paled, clenched their teeth and loaded their guns. Just as it looked as if events might take a tragic turn, Don Camillo raised his hand.

"Stop!" he shouted. "I'm coming to open the door."

When he came to open it the committee was ready. There were thirty members in all—Peppone and his councilmen and the police sergeant with four of his men. They made a mercilessly thorough search, opening every chest of drawers and cupboard and cabinet, tapping the walls and floors, sounding every bottle and barrel in the cellar and exploring under the eaves, up the chimney, and in the woodhouse. Even if anything so small as a needle had been the object of their search, they would surely have found it. All the food they turned up in the kitchen amounted to three eggs, a loaf of bread, and a rind of cheese. And in the cellar, two salami sausages and two gourds full of lard hanging from the ceiling. Don Camillo stood by with folded arms and an indifferent air. After they had fingered the mattresses they said they wanted to examine the bell tower and the church. The sergeant turned pale, but Don Camillo led the way, and let the committee look into the sacristy and the confessionals and under the altar. They did not touch anything, but insisted upon nosing everywhere. Finally, with nothing to show for their pains, they left the house, with their heads hanging. They conferred for a while with the crowd, and finally the latter melted away.

Don Camillo ate no supper either. He lay for a while on his bed, gazing up at the beams of the ceiling, then when he could see them no longer he went into the church and knelt before the altar.

"Lord, I thank You," he murmured.

But there was no reply. Now whenever this happened Don Camillo acquired a fever and went on a diet of bread and water and went for days and days, until Christ felt sorry for him and said: "enough." But this time he hadn't had even bread and water so he went back to his room. There were two windows in this room; one looked out on the village square and the other on the rectory garden. The latter was still wide open, and hanging out of it was a blanket that had been put there to dry earlier in the day. He pulled the blanket in, revealing three nails in the outside wall of the house, each one with a Tommy gun strung to it. He pulled in the guns and put them in a sack. Then he went down to the cellar and took down one of the two sausages and the gourds. Only one of the sausages was stuffed with pork, and both gourds contained heavy yellow grease with cartridges embedded in it. He added the false sausage and the gourds to his sack, climbed over the garden hedge and walked across the fields until he came to the river. There he got into a boat, rowed out past that spit of land

:[44]:

known locally as the Island and threw the sack into the water. After which, he went back to kneel in front of the altar.

"I thank You, Lord," he whispered again. "I thank You for not having let them find the things I have just thrown away. Those are what they were after. They wanted to make a sensational story out of their discovery. I thank You not for my sake, but for having saved the reputation of the Church."

"Very well, Don Camillo. But I told you many times before to throw those things away."

Don Camillo sighed.

"Here I am, stripped of everything, with only an old shotgun that would scare nothing bigger than an owl for a weapon. How am I to defend myself?"

"With your honesty, Don Camillo."

"No," said the priest. "You saw today for Yourself that honesty is no defense. Peppone and his gang knew what they were really looking for, but the others shouted against me just because of a false accusation intended to persuade them that I was a thief. My honesty was no help at all. And it won't do any good in the future. They don't know I've got rid of the guns, and because they were thwarted in their plan to disgrace me they'll continue their war to the knife against me. But I'll . . ."

He threw out his chest and clenched his big fists. Then he relaxed, lowered his head and bowed low.

"I'll do nothing at all. The lie has been sown by now, and I'm known as 'the priest who grows fat on the food of the poor'."

As he said this, the thought came to him that he hadn't eaten all day and so he closed the church for the night and went to the rectory cellar. There he reached for the genuine sausage with the intention of eating a slice or two of it for a late supper. But his knife struck something hard.

"I threw the good salami away with the guns, and here I am

with one full of cartridges," he said to himself with a melancholy smile.

After a sad meal consisting of a rind of cheese he went to bed. Meanwhile, in the darkness of his own room, Peppone was thinking of the meager contents of Don Camillo's cupboard: three eggs, a loaf of bread, and a piece of cheese. He turned over and over in his bed, unable to close his eyes. Then he remembered the two sausages hanging in the cellar. "Well, he'll have a bite of sausage," he muttered to himself, and went to sleep with an easy conscience.

THE POLAR PACT

THOSE WERE THE DAYS
when there was a great deal of racket about that piece of
international political machinery known as the "Atlantic
Pact," which may have owed its name to the fact that between
words and deeds there lies the breadth of an ocean. Peppone
took the whole proposition as a personal insult. He was so
thoroughly incensed by the American "saboteurs of peace"
that if it had been within his power he would have declared
war upon the United States without an instant's delay. He
was in this state of boiling frenzy when he saw Don Camillo

pass by, with his nose in his breviary, and from the workshop door threw at him an oath violent enough to make anyone's hair stand up on end.

Don Camillo stopped and raised his eyes. "Did you call me?" he asked mildly.

"I was speaking to God," said Peppone threateningly. "Do you think you are the Deity in person?"

"No, I don't. But since God hasn't time to listen to you, say what you have to say to me."

Although Peppone was raring to declare war on the United States, he didn't want to open hostilities with an attack upon Don Camillo, who was standing all too close by and was holding in one hand a piece of steel cable he had just picked up from the ground. There was no point to being blessed by a priest who wielded such a holy water sprinkler, so he contented himself with shrugging his shoulders. Fortunately, at this very moment, a tractor clanked up and came to a halt between them, and Peppone turned his attention to the driver's tale of woe.

"There's something wrong," said the driver. "The motor spits and kicks back. It must be the timing."

Now Peppone, in addition to being mayor, was the village mechanic—in fact he was the best mechanic within miles. He could work wonders with machinery of all kinds, but in this case the tractor was a Fordson and Peppone looked at it with distaste, pointing the handle of his hammer at the plate bearing the words "Made In U. S. A."

"The U. S. A. and I are through with each other," he said. "If you want to get this piece of junk fixed, go see the priest. He's the one that's in with the Americans."

Don Camillo had just resumed his walk, but he turned back slowly. He peeled off his overcoat and gave it, along with his hat and breviary, to the driver. Then he rolled up his sleeves and began to tinker with the motor.

"Give me a pair of pincers," he said and the driver got one out of his tool-box. Don Camillo worked a few minutes longer and then stood up straight. "Start it going," he said.

The man stepped on the starter.

"Like clockwork," he said happily. "How much do I owe you, Father, for your trouble?"

"Not a penny," said Don Camillo. "It's included in the Marshall Plan!"

A moment later the tractor pulled away. Peppone was left gaping, and Don Camillo opened his breviary under his nose.

"Read this and tell me what it means," he said, pointing to a sentence on the page.

Peppone shrugged his shoulders.

"My Latin won't take me that far," he mumbled.

"Then you're a donkey," Don Camillo said calmly, continuing his walk. He had got grease up his nose, but he was proud of it.

This incident was a trifling matter, but it put Peppone in a very bad humor. That evening, when he had gathered his stalwarts together in the People's Palace, he shouted that something must be done to show the indignation of the masses over the signing of the infamous Atlantic Pact.

"We must take over and occupy some important place," he exclaimed in conclusion. "It's got to be a spectacular protest."

"Chief," said Smilzo, "we already occupy the People's Palace and the town hall. Our children occupy the school and our dead the cemetery. All that's left for us to occupy is the church."

"Thanks!" said Peppone. "And if we occupy it, what do we do next? Say Masses to compete with those of the Vatican? No, we must occupy a place that will benefit the whole people. Brusco, do you get what I mean?"

Brusco caught on at once.

"Good," he said. "When do we start moving?"

"Right away. Before midnight all our people must be put on the alert. They must move in waves, beginning at two o'clock, and by five the whole Island must be ours."

Just at the village the river broadened to such an extent that it seemed like a patch of sea, and there lay the place known as the Island. It was not an island, really, but a strip of land fifty feet offshore running parallel, for about half a mile, to the mainland and attached to it at the lower end by a spit or tongue of muddy earth almost submerged by water. The Island was not cultivated but was given over to a grove of poplars. That is, the poplars grew of their own accord, and every now and then the owner, Signor Bresca, came to mark with a knife those which were to be cut down and sold.

Peppone and his followers had said for some time that this was a typical example of abandoned and neglected private property and that it ought to be turned over to the workers for development as a coöperative farm. Its occupation had been put off from one day to another, but now the time had come.

"We'll oppose the 'Atlantic Pact' with a 'Polar Pact' of our own!" Peppone exclaimed on the evening of this historical decision.

It seems that, in spite of appearances, the word "Polar" in this case was derived from the river Po. It was a strictly local and proletarian term, with no reactionary Latin pedigree. Surely it was time to do away with Julius Caesar, and the ancient Romans, who together with the clergy used Latin to pull the wool over the people's eyes. At least, this was Peppone's answer to someone who objected on etymological grounds to his idea of giving a Party newspaper the name of "The Polà Call."

"The days of etymology are over," Peppone told him. "Every word is making a fresh start."

In any case, the "Polar Pact" was put into action, and at seven o'clock the next morning Don Camillo was warned that Peppone and his men had occupied the Island. The "men" were actually for the most part women but, be that as it may, they were cutting down poplars as fast as they could, one after another. One tree, higher than the rest, had been plucked like a chicken neck and now served as a pole from which the Red Flag fluttered happily in the April breeze.

"There's going to be trouble," the messenger told Don Camillo. "Someone's called for special police from the city. Peppone has started to cut the connecting spit of land and says he'll hold out there indefinitely. If you don't do something there's no telling where the trouble will end."

Don Camillo pulled on a pair of rough twill trousers, rubber boots and a hunter's jacket, for he knew that the Island was a sea of mud.

Peppone was on the spot, standing with his legs far apart, directing the cutting of the channel. At first he failed to recognize Don Camillo; then he pretended not to; but in the end he couldn't help bursting out with: "Did you disguise yourself so as to spy on the enemy's camp?"

Don Camillo came down from the river bank, plunged halfway up his legs into the mud, crossed the channel and arrived in front of Peppone.

"Drop all that, Peppone," he pleaded; "the police are on their way from the city."

"Let them come!" Peppone answered. "If they want to get over here, they'll have to borrow the United States Navy!"

"Peppone, it's only fifteen yards from the shore to the Island, and bullets can travel."

"It's only fifteen yards from the Island to the shore, for that

:[51]:

matter," said Peppone somberly, "and we have bullets too."

Peppone was really in a bad fix, and Don Camillo knew it.

"Listen," he said, pulling him to one side, "you have a right to be a fool and behave like one if you want to. But you have no right to involve these other poor devils in your folly. If you want to be sent up to the penitentiary, stand your ground and shoot. But you can't compel the rest of them to be sent up with you."

Peppone thought for a minute or two and then shouted: "The others can do as they please. I'm not forcing anybody. Those who want to stick it out can stay."

The men who were digging the channel stopped and leaned on their shovels. They could hear a roar of motors from the main road.

"The jeeps of the special police," Don Camillo said in a loud voice. And the men looked at Peppone.

"Do as you please," Peppone muttered. "Democracy allows every man to follow his own will. And here on the Island we have democracy!"

Just then Smilzo and the other Comrades arrived upon the scene. Smilzo shot a curious glance at Don Camillo.

"Is the Vatican sticking its nose into things again?" he asked. "You'd better make yourself scarce, Father; it's going to be hot around here."

"Heat doesn't bother me," Don Camillo answered.

A cloud of dust rose from the road.

"They're here," said the shovelers. With which they threw down their shovels and made their way ashore. Peppone looked at them with scorn.

There were six jeeps in all, and the police lieutenant stood up and called out to the men who were hacking at the underbrush on the Island: "Move on!"

They went on hacking, and the lieutenant turned to one of his aides.

"Perhaps they didn't hear," he said. "Play some music!"

His aide fired a volley of shots into the air, and the Islanders raised their heads.

"Get moving!" the lieutenant shouted.

Peppone and his henchmen grouped themselves at one end of the channel. Some of the men who had been working behind them crossed over. When they reached the shore they scattered to right and left, skirting the jeeps that were in their way. About a dozen die-hards continued to cut down the underbrush. Peppone and his men fell into line, forming a wall along the canal, and stood there with folded arms, waiting.

"Move on! Vacate!" came a shout from the bank.

No one budged, and the police got out of their jeeps and started down the river bank.

The veins of Peppone's neck were swollen and his jaw was set. "The first one to lay hands on me will get strangled," he said darkly.

Don Camillo was still there beside him, forming part of the living wall.

"For the love of God, Peppone," he murmured, "don't do anything rash."

"What are you doing here?" Peppone asked him, startled.

"Doing my duty. I'm here to remind you that you're a thinking being and therefore have got to think things out clearly. Come on, let's go!"

"Go ahead! I've never run away in my life, and I never will."

"But this is the law!"

"It's your law, not mine. Go on and obey it."

The police were down beside the river, just across from the Island.

"Vacate!" they shouted.

Don Camillo tugged at Peppone's sleeve.

"Let's go!"

"I won't move out of here alive. And the first one to lay hands on me gets his skull cracked!"

The police repeated their injunction and then began walking through the mud. When they came up against the wall of men they repeated it again, but no one moved or gave any answer.

A sergeant grabbed hold of Peppone's jacket and would have come to a very bad end if Don Camillo hadn't pinned Peppone's arms down from behind.

"Let go!" he muttered between his clenched teeth.

Don Camillo had on the same sort of trousers and boots and jacket as the rest, and when the police started laying about them he got one of the first blows and was sorely tempted to let Peppone go, and to pitch some of the attackers into the water. Instead, he took it without batting an eyelash. More blows fell on his head and on those of Smilzo and the others. But no one said a word. They held on to each other and took it in silence. Finally, they had to be hauled away like rocks, but none of them had opened his mouth or moved a finger in revolt.

"They're crazy in this village," the lieutenant grumbled. By now the Island was empty, because the few men who were left had escaped in boats. The police got into their jeeps and drove away.

Don Camillo, Peppone, and the others sat silently on the shore, gazing into the water and at the Red Flag waving from the plucked poplar.

"Father, you've got a bump as big as a walnut on your forehead," said Smilzo.

"You don't need to tell me," said Don Camillo. "I can feel it."

They got up and went back to the village, and that was the end of the "Polar Pact."

THE PETITION

 D ON CAMILLO WAS WALK-
ing quietly along the Low Road toward the village, smoking
his usual cigar when, just around a curve, he came upon
Peppone's gang. There were five of them, and Smilzo was in
charge. Don Camillo looked at them with frank curiosity.

"Are you planning to bump me off?" he asked them. "Or
have you some better place in mind?"

"Don't you dare incite us to violence!" said Smilzo, taking
a sheet of paper out of an envelope and unfolding it before
him.

"Is this for the last wishes of the condemned man?"

"It's for everyone that wants peace to sign," said Smilzo. "If you don't sign, then you don't want peace. From now on, honest men and warmongers are going to be clearly divided."

Don Camillo examined the dove printed at the top of the paper.

"I'm an honest man," he said, "but I'm not signing. A man that wants peace doesn't have to testify to it with his signature."

Smilzo turned to Gigo, who was standing beside him.

"He thinks this is a political move," he said. "According to him, everything we do is tied up with politics."

"Look, there's no politics in this," put in Gigo. "It's just a question of preserving peace. Peace is good for all political parties. It will take a lot of signatures to get us out of the Atlantic Pact, and if we don't get out, it's going to get us into a war, as sure as shooting."

Don Camillo shook the ashes off the end of his cigar.

"You'd better get going," he said. "If I'm not mistaken, you haven't even started."

"Of course not. We wanted you to have the honor of being the first name on the list. That's only natural. When peace is at stake, the clergy ought to take the lead."

Don Camillo threw out his arms. "It can be taken for granted that the clergy's in favor of peace, so it's just as if my signature were there."

"Then you're not going to sign?"

Don Camillo shook his head and walked away.

"If we're saddled with a clergy of this kind, then we'll have to fight not one war but two," Smilzo said bitterly, putting the paper back in the envelope.

A little later, Peppone arrived at the rectory door.

"No politics involved," he declared. "I'm here in the

capacities of mayor, citizen, father of a family, Christian, and honest man."

"Too many people!" exclaimed Don Camillo. "Too big a crowd! Come in just as Peppone, and leave the rest outside."

Peppone came in and sat down.

"We've come to the ragged edge," he began. "If honest men don't stick together, the world's headed for a smash-up."

"Sorry to hear it," Don Camillo answered seriously. "Is there anything new?"

"Only that if we don't safeguard peace, everything's going to pieces. Let's leave politics and parties out of it and all get together."

Don Camillo nodded. "That's the way I like to hear you talk," he said. "It's about time you cut loose from that brood of Satan."

"I said we'd leave politics out of it," retorted Peppone. "This is a time for thinking in worldwide terms."

Don Camillo looked at him with astonishment, for he had never heard him mouth such big words.

"Do you want peace or don't you?" asked Peppone. "Are you with Jesus Christ or against Him?"

"You know the answer."

Out of his pocket Peppone took the envelope and paper Don Camillo had seen earlier in the day.

"When it comes to fighting for peace, the clergy must be in the front line," he asserted.

Don Camillo shook his head. "You're changing the rules of the game. Didn't you say politics wasn't in it?"

"I'm here as a plain citizen," Peppone insisted.

"Very well then, as one citizen to another, I tell you I'm not biting." And as Peppone started to rise excitedly to his feet, he added: "You know very well that if I sign your paper, a lot of other signatures will follow. Without me, you can only hope for those of your own people, and a lot of them can't write their own names. Since you see that I'm not to be taken in, put that pigeon back in your pocket and hand me two glasses from the sideboard. Otherwise, you and your pigeon and your cause of peace may as well all go back where you came from."

Peppone tucked the paper away.

"Since you're giving yourself such airs," he said proudly, "I'll show you that I can get all the signatures I want without yours as an attraction."

Smilzo and the rest of the "peace gang" were waiting outside.

"Start making the rounds," said Peppone. "But go to our people last. Everyone's got to sign. Peace must be defended, with blows, if necessary."

"Chief, if I go to jail, what will happen?" Smilzo asked him.

"Nothing will happen. A man can serve the cause perfectly well in jail."

These words were not exactly comforting. But Smilzo set out, with the gang at his heels, strengthened by some reën-forcements from the People's Palace.

Now when people have haystacks and vineyards and fields, it's almost impossible for them to say no to a fellow who asks them to sign up for peace and swears politics doesn't enter into it. And in a village the first five or six signatures are what count. It took several evenings to cover the whole area. But there were no arguments, except from Tonini, who shook his head when they showed him the paper.

"Don't you want peace?"

"No," said Tonini, who was a fellow with hands as big as shovels. "I happen to like war. It kills off a lot of rascals and clears the air."

Here Smilzo made a very sensible observation.

"But you know, of course, that more honest men are killed off than rascals."

"But I care even less for honest men."

"And what if you get killed yourself?"

"I'd rather be killed than sign a paper. At least, when you die, you know where you're going."

The gang started to come forward, but Tonini picked up his shotgun, and Smilzo said he needn't bother.

Everything else went smoothly, and when Peppone saw the sheets full of signatures, he was so happy that he brought his fist down on the table hard enough to make the People's Palace tremble. He compared the peace list with the village census and found that they tallied. The mayors of the neighboring villages complained that they couldn't get people to sign because the reactionaries obstructed them. There had been shooting at Castellina and fisticuffs at Fossa for a whole day. And to think that Smilzo, after taking an hour to persuade each of the first five or six signatories, had won over the rest without a murmur.

"It's the prestige I enjoy as mayor," said Peppone, and he gathered together the papers and went to savor his triumph.

Don Camillo was reading a book when Peppone appeared before him.

"The power of the clergy is on the decline!" Peppone announced to him. "I thank you in the name of the world's democracies for not having signed. Your signature wouldn't have have brought in half as many others. It's too bad for the Pope, that's all." And he added, spreading his papers out on the table, "America's done for! The Atlantic Pact is no good, because we have a totality of votes against it. And everywhere else it's going to be the same way."

Don Camillo scrutinized the lists carefully. Then he threw out his arms. "I'm sorry to tell you, but one signature is missing. Tonini's. So you can't claim a 'totality'."

Peppone laughed.

"I have all the rest," he said. "What's one against eight hundred?"

Don Camillo opened a drawer, took out some papers, and scattered them in front of Peppone.

"You have signatures against the Pact and I have signatures in its favor."

Peppone opened his eyes wide.

"Russia's done for," said Don Camillo. "Because I have Tonini's signature along with the rest."

Peppone scratched his head.

"There's nothing so remarkable about it," Don Camillo pointed out. "I worked by day, and your men went around by night, when people were already softened up. As a matter of fact, they were glad to sign for you, because that cancelled their signing for me. The only one who didn't like it was Tonini, because I had to knock his head against a wall. But I advise you not to go after him, because he says that before he'll sign another petition he'll shoot to kill."

Peppone took his papers away. And so it was that in Don Camillo's village, America triumphed by one to zero, all on account of Tonini.

A SOLOMON
COME TO JUDGMENT

ONE DAY, AFTER DON
Camillo and Peppone had settled a slight misunderstanding
to the mutual satisfaction of both, the mayor turned to the
priest and said, "There's no sense in turning everything in
life into a tragedy. If we reason things out, we can always
compromise."

"Right you are," said Don Camillo warmly. "Why did God
give us brains if He didn't expect us to reason?"

The two men parted on this note, and a few days later something happened in the valley which clearly proves that man is a reasoning creature, especially when it comes to living peacefully with his neighbor. First, however, you need to know the local geography of the little world or you won't understand a thing about it.

The Po river rolls on its mighty way without so much as an if-you-please and on either side it is fed by countless streams and tributaries. The Tincone is one of these little streams. Now the Molinetto road, running parallel to the Po, connects the tiny communities of Pieve and La Rocca. At a certain point the road crosses the Tincone. Here there is a bridge; it is, in fact, a structure of some size because at this point the Tincone is fairly wide, being only a mile or so away from where it flows into the big river. Pieve and La Rocca are each about three miles from the bridge over the Tincone which is, indeed, the boundary line between them.

This is the topography of the story, and its point of departure is the problem of public education. The school that served both communities was at La Rocca, and for the people of Pieve this was a serious matter. Every day their children had to travel six miles, and six miles are thirty thousand feet, even in the flat river valley. Children can't resist taking shortcuts, and since the road they traveled was straight as an arrow, the shortcuts always led them a longer way around.

One day a committee of women from Pieve came to the mayor of the whole township, Peppone, and announced that unless they were given a schoolhouse of their own, they wouldn't send their children to school. Now the township was about as rich as a traveling rabbit and a new school would have entailed not only building costs but double the amount of teachers' salaries as well. So, having by hook or crook raised some funds, Peppone decided to build the new schoolhouse at the bridge over the Tincone, halfway between Pieve and La

:[62]:

Rocca, and send the children from both communities there. But at this point the problem became thorny.

"That's all very well," they said at La Rocca, "as long as it's on our side of the bridge."

"All well and good," they said at Pieve, "but of course it must be on our side."

To be exact, both of them were in the wrong (or in the right, as you prefer), because the real halfway point was not on either side of the bridge but in the middle.

"You don't want the school built on the bridge, do you?" Peppone shouted, after a long discussion with committees from both villages.

"You're the mayor," they answered, "and it's up to you to find a fair solution."

"The only real solution would be to lead you all to the bridge, tie millstones around your necks and throw you into the water," said Peppone. And he wasn't so wrong either.

"It's not a question of a hundred yards one way or the other," they told him. "Social justice is at stake." And that silenced the mayor very effectively, because whenever he heard the phrase "social justice," Peppone drew himself up as if he were witnessing the miracle of creation.

Meanwhile trouble began to brew. Some boys from La Rocca went by night to the bridge and painted a red line across the middle. Then they announced that anyone from Pieve would find it healthier to stay on his own side. The next evening, boys from Pieve painted a green line parallel to the red one and intimated that anyone from La Rocca would be better off at home. The third evening, boys from both villages arrived at the middle of the bridge at the same time. One of those from La Rocca spat over the green line and one of those from Pieve spat over the red one. A quarter of an hour later, three boys were in the river and five had severe wounds on the head. The worst of it was that of the three boys in the river, two were from Pieve and only one was from La Rocca, so to even up the score another boy from La Rocca would have to be thrown in. And of the five boys with head wounds, three were from La Rocca and two from Pieve and so another boy from Pieve needed a beating. All, of course, for the sake of social justice.

The number of head wounds and boys thrown into the river increased daily, and soon the numbers were swelled by grown men, both old and young. Then one day Smilzo, who hung about the bridge as an observer, brought Peppone a piece of really bad news.

"There's been a fist fight between a woman from Pieve and a woman from La Rocca."

Now when women get mixed up in an affair of this kind, the trouble really starts. Women are always the ones to stick a gun into the hand of husband, brother, lover, father or son. Women are the plague of politics, and alas, politics is about ninety-five percent of the world's occupation. So it was that knives were drawn and shots began to fly.

"Something's got to be done," said Peppone, "or else we won't need a school but a cemetery."

Aside from the fact that there's more to be learned in the cool tomb than in a school room, this was no joking matter, and Peppone handled it in masterful fashion. Out on the Po there had lain for years an old floating water mill, made of two big hulks with the millwheel between and a cabin bridging them over. Peppone had these towed under the central arch of the bridge across the Tincone. He chained them to the supporting columns and then remodeled them in such a way as to make them into one, joined by gangplanks to both banks of the river. So it was that one day there was a solemn opening of the new floating school. A large crowd was present, including a group of newspapermen from the big city.

The only accident ever recorded took place when Beletti, a boy who had to repeat the third grade for six years in succession, threw his teacher into the water. But this did not upset Peppone.

"Italy is in the middle of the Mediterranean," he said, "and everybody must know how to swim."

PEPPONE'S PASSION TO show moving-pictures was inherited straight from his father. His father, too, was mechanically minded, and he had brought the first threshing-machine to the Valley, as all the old inhabitants remembered very well. Young people may laugh, because they fail to see any connection between moving pictures and a threshing-machine. But the young people of today are benighted creatures born with their telephone numbers imprinted on their brains, and where passion is concerned they have about as much grace as a pig in a cornfield.

In the old days electric power was a luxury confined to the city, and since a moving-picture projector has to be run electrically, country people had no chance to see any pictures. But Peppone's father mounted a dynamo on the steam engine that powered the thresher, and when his machine wasn't needed in the fields he hitched two oxen to it and went from village to village, giving picture shows. So many years have gone by that the young people of today can't possibly visualize a steam engine drawn by two oxen. It was painted green with magnificent bands of shiny brass around it and had an enormous fly-wheel and a tall smokestack, which was lowered while it was traveling from one place to another. It didn't smell or make any noise, and it had a very wonderful whistle.

So Peppone's ambition to show moving-pictures was quite legitimately in his blood. As soon as the auditorium of the newly built "People's Palace" was at his disposal, this was the first thing that came into his mind. One fine morning the village awoke to find itself plastered with posters announcing the opening of the moving-picture season at the People's Palace the next Sunday.

Now Don Camillo's father had never even thought about going around the countryside to show moving-pictures, but for some time Don Camillo had been set upon the idea of acquiring a projector for his Recreation Center and Peppone's announcement made his stomach turn over. He was somewhat consoled on Sunday by a fierce storm and a floodlike downpour of rain. At ten o'clock in the evening he was still waiting to hear what had happened when his friend Barchini, dripping but happy, appeared at the door.

"There were only a few waifs and strays at the People's Palace," Barchini told him. "The rain kept the people from the outskirts away. What's more, the lights kept going on and off, and finally they had to stop the show. Peppone was fit to be tied."

Don Camillo went to kneel before Christ on the altar.

"Lord, I thank You . . ." he began.

"What for, Don Camillo?"

"For sending a storm and disrupting the electric current."

"Don Camillo, I had nothing to do with the lights going off. I'm a carpenter, not an electrician. And as for the storm, do you really think that Almighty God would inconvenience winds, clouds, lightning and thunder simply in order to prevent Peppone from showing his pictures?"

Don Camillo lowered his head.

"No, I don't really think so," he stammered. "We men have a way of thanking God for anything that falls in with our plans, as if it had come to pass just for our pleasure."

At midnight the storm died down, but at three o'clock in the morning it came back more fiercely than before, and an unearthly noise awakened Don Camillo. He had never heard a crash so loud and so close, and when he reached the window and looked out he was left gaping. The spire of the church tower had been struck by lightning and shattered into pieces. It was just as simple as all that, but to Don Camillo it was so incredible that he rushed to tell Christ about it.

"Lord," he said in a voice shaky with emotion, "the church spire has been struck by lightning."

"I understand, Don Camillo," Christ answered calmly. "Buildings are often struck that way in the course of a storm."

"But this was the church!" Don Camillo insisted.

"I heard you, Don Camillo."

Don Camillo looked up at the crucified Christ and threw out his arms in dismay.

"Why did it have to happen?" he asked bitterly.

"A church spire has been struck by lightning in the course of a storm," said Christ. "Does God have to justify Himself for this in your sight? A short time ago you thanked Him for sending a storm that damaged your neighbor, and now you reproach Him because the same storm has damaged you."

"It hasn't damaged me," said Don Camillo. "It has damaged the house of God."

"The house of God is infinite and eternal. Even if every planet in the universe were to be reduced to dust, the house of God would still stand. A church spire has been struck by lightning, that is all anyone is entitled to think or say. The lightning had to strike somewhere."

Don Camillo was talking to Christ but during the conversation the thought of the mutilated tower was uppermost in his mind.

"Surely that particular stroke could have stayed away," he said. And Christ took pity on his sorrow and continued to reason gently with him.

"Calm yourself, Don Camillo, and think it out clearly. God created the universe, and the universe is a perfect and harmonious system, in which every element is indissolubly bound, whether directly or indirectly, to all the rest. Everything that happens in the universe is necessary and foreordained, and if this stroke of lightning had not fallen exactly where and when it did, the harmony of the universe would have been troubled. This harmony is perfect, and if the lightning struck at this time and place, then it is a meet and right thing and we must thank God for it. We must thank Him for everything that takes place in the universe, for everything is a proof of His infallibility and the perfection of His creation. The stroke of lightning had to fall just where it did and not an inch in any other direction. The fault is man's, for having chosen to build the tower in that place. He could quite as well have built it a couple of yards farther over."

Don Camillo thought of his mutilated tower and there was bitterness in his heart.

"If everything that happens in the universe is foreordained and a manifestation of God's will, and otherwise the system would not be perfect, then the church tower had to be built where it is and not a couple of yards farther over."

"Yes, it could have been built a couple of yards farther over," Christ answered with a smile, "but then man would unconsciously have violated God's law. And that God didn't allow."

"Then there's no free will," protested Don Camillo.

Christ continued to smile and to speak in the same gentle tone.

"Woe to the man who out of anger or grief or sensual excitement forgets those things that deep down inside he cannot help but know. God points out the right way, but man has a choice whether to follow it or not. In His infinite kindness God leaves man free to choose the wrong way and yet, by repentance and recognition of his mistake, to save his soul. A church spire has been struck by lightning in the course of a storm. The lightning had to strike there, and so the man who built the tower is to blame. Yet the tower had to be built where it is and man must thank God for it."

Don Camillo sighed.

"Lord, I thank You. But if with Your help I manage to put up another spire, I am going to arm it with a lightning rod."

"Yes, Don Camillo, if it is foreordained that you are to put a lightning rod on the tower, then you will surely do so."

Don Camillo bowed his head. Then in the first light of dawn he climbed up to examine the damaged tower more closely.

"Exactly," he said to himself at last. "The tower had to be built just where it is!"

Soon people began to crowd into the square to see the tower. They stood there in the torrential rain and looked at it in bewilderment, without speaking. When the square was full, Peppone and his crew appeared on the scene. He pushed his way to the front of the crowd and stood there for some time staring at the sight. Then he solemnly pointed one finger to the sky.

"Here is a proof of God's wrath!" he exclaimed. "This is God's answer to your boycott. Lightning strikes where God wills, and God wills it to accomplish a purpose."

Don Camillo listened from the rectory window. Peppone spied him there and pointed him out to the crowd.

"The priest is silent," he shouted, "because the lightning struck his church. If it had struck our People's Palace, he'd have plenty to say."

Smilzo looked up at Don Camillo too.

"This is God's answer to the warmongers!" he shouted. "Hurrah for Mao-tse-tung!"

"Hurrah for peace and the Confederation of Labor!" chorused his followers.

Don Camillo counted to fifty-two before saying what was boiling up inside him. Then he said nothing. He took a half-smoked cigar out of his pocket and lit it.

"Look at that!" shouted Peppone. "Nero fiddling while Carthage burns!"

With which slightly garbled historical reference, he and his gang stalked proudly away.

Toward evening Don Camillo took his bitterness to the altar.

"Lord," he said at the end of his prayer, "what maddens me is to hear those scoundrels speak of Your divine wrath. I wouldn't dream of destroying the harmony of the universe, but after the blasphemous things they said this morning it would serve them right if lightning were to strike their People's Palace. Their blasphemies were enough to provoke divine wrath in earnest!"

"You're going in for pretty loose talk yourself, Don Camillo," said Christ with a smile. "Have you the nerve to inconvenience God in all His majesty just in order to knock down the four walls of a village shack? You must respect your God more than that, Don Camillo!"

Don Camillo went back to the rectory. The distance was a short one, but at night, even within the space of a few steps, there's no telling what may happen. It was still raining, and at midnight the rain was coming down harder than ever. At one o'clock the stormy cacophony of the night before was repeated, and at two a clap of thunder aroused the whole village. By two-ten everyone was awake, because a building on the square was afire, and the building was the People's Palace. When Don Camillo arrived the square was crowded with people, but Smilzo and his followers had already extinguished the flames. The roof had caved in, most of the framework was destroyed and the rest was a heap of smoldering ashes. Don Camillo edged up as if by accident to Peppone.

"A neat job," he observed casually. "Lightning seems to have a conscience."

Peppone wheeled around.

"Have half a cigar?" said Don Camillo.

"I don't smoke," answered Peppone darkly.

"You're quite right. The People's Palace is doing enough smoking. But I'm sorry. If you don't smoke, how can I say 'Nero fiddling while Carthage burns?' Only, for your information, it wasn't Carthage, it was Rome."

"That's good news! With every priest in it, I trust!"

Don Camillo shook his head and said gravely and in a loud voice: "You mustn't provoke God's wrath. Don't you see

:[72]:

what you've brought upon yourself with the sacrilegious words you uttered this morning?"

Peppone almost jumped out of his skin with rage.

"Don't lose your temper," Don Camillo advised him; "the Marshall Plan might help you out."

Peppone stood face to face with Don Camillo, his fists clenched.

"The roof will be fixed in a few days," he shouted. "We don't need any plans; we'll take care of it ourselves."

"Good for you, Mr. Mayor," said Don Camillo, dropping his voice. "That way you can kill two birds with one stone. When you get the Council to appropriate money for the People's Palace, you can allot something for the repair of the church tower as well."

"Over my dead body!" said Peppone. "Ask your Americans for that. The People's Palace is a public utility, and the church is a private corporation."

Don Camillo lit the butt of his cigar.

"It was quite a stroke of lightning," he observed, "much more powerful than mine. It made a magnificent noise and did quite a bit of damage. Someone really ought to study it from a scientific point of view. I think I'll speak to the police sergeant about it."

"Keep your nose in your own dirty business," said Peppone.

"My business is to get you to repair the church tower."

Peppone shot him a somber look.

"All right," he said between clenched teeth. "But some day I'll settle accounts with you."

Don Camillo started back to the rectory. There was nothing more to see or to say. He meant to go straight home, but he knew that Christ was waiting for him.

"Don Camillo," said Christ severely, when the priest stood

:[73]:

before him in the half-dark church. "Aren't you going to thank Me because the People's Palace was struck by lightning?"

"No," said Don Camillo, with his head hanging. "A stroke of lightning is part of the natural order created by God. Surely God wouldn't inconvenience wind, clouds, lightning and thunder simply in order to please a poor devil of a country priest and knock down the walls of a village shack."

"Exactly," said Christ, "and how could God take advantage of a storm to throw a bomb on the roof of the People's Palace? Only a poor devil of a country priest could think up a thing like that."

Don Camillo held out his arms.

"Yes, Lord, but even in this shameful deed there is evidence of God's mercy. If the poor devil of a country priest, tempted by Satan himself, hadn't tossed a bomb on the roof of the People's Palace, then the case of dynamite hidden in the Palace attic wouldn't have exploded, and its presence there was a menace. Now the menace has been eliminated and the poor devil of a country priest has found a way to have the spire of his church tower properly replaced. Moreover, an individual who took the Lord's name in vain has received the punishment he deserved."

"Don Camillo," said Christ, "are you sure you did the right thing?"

"No," Don Camillo replied. "God leaves man free to choose between right and wrong. I did wrong, I admit it, and I shall repent."

"Aren't you repentant already?"

"No, Lord," whispered Don Camillo. "It's still too early. I must ask for an extension."

Christ sighed, and Don Camillo went off to bed. In spite of his guilty conscience he slept like a log and dreamed that there was a gleaming gold spire on the church tower. When he woke up, he thought happily of his dream. But he realized that he had forgotten one very important thing. So he dropped off to sleep again and dreamed that on the gleaming spire there was a wonderful lightning rod.

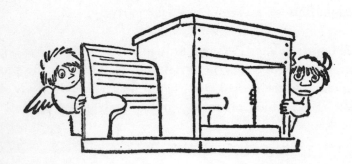

B ARCHINI, THE VILLAGE
printer and stationer, had been ill for some time, and there
was no one to replace him in the shop, for his was the sort
of business where "boss" and "working class" are combined
in one and the same person. So it was that Don Camillo had
to hire someone in the city to print his parish magazine, and
when he went back to read the proofs he amused himself by
poking about among the machines.

The devil is a rascal who has no respect for anything or
anybody, and plays his tricks not only in night-clubs and

:[76]:

other so-called resorts of perdition, but also in places where honest men are at work. In this case, the devil was lurking near the machine where a man was printing letterheads, and when Don Camillo got out on the street he found himself in a pretty pickle. Since the flesh is notoriously weak and even the most honorable of parish priests has some flesh and blood in his make-up, what was Don Camillo to do when, upon his return to the village, he found his pockets stuffed with five or six sheets of writing paper, bearing the address of the provincial headquarters of a certain political party?

A few days later Peppone was surprised to receive a registered letter with a city postmark and on the back the name Franchini, which he had never heard before. Inside, there was a letterhead which made him instinctively draw himself to attention.

Dear Comrade:
  Of course, you are already acquainted with the latest American betrayal, a secret clause in the nefarious Atlantic Pact which compels the other conspiring nations to watch over their democratic parties and sabotage any efforts on behalf of peace. Since we are under watch by the police, it is folly to put our Party name on our envelopes, that is, except when we actually want to have the police find out about something. When the time comes you will receive detailed rules for the conduct of your correspondence.
  We are writing you today about a delicate and strictly confidential matter. Comrade, the capitalists and clergy are working for war. Peace is under attack, and the Soviet Union, which alone has the benevolent power to defend it, needs the help of active friends.
  The Soviet Union must be ready to bear the onslaught which the Western World is preparing to launch against it. The sacred cause of Peace needs men of unshakeable faith and professional ability, ready to discipline themselves for action. We are so sure of you, Comrade, that the Special

Committee for Political Action has unanimously decided to admit you to the inner sanctum. Here is a piece of news that should fill you with pride and joy: you are to be sent to the Soviet Union, where your mechanical talents will be put to work in the cause of Peace.

The Socialist Homeland will accord to the members of the Peace Brigade the rights and privileges of a Soviet citizen. We call this to your attention as one more sign of our Soviet comrades' generosity.

Instructions as to the day of departure and the equipment you should take with you will follow. You will travel by air. In view of the delicacy of this matter, we order you to destroy this letter and to send your reply to the comrade whose name and address are on the envelope. Take good care. Today more than ever, the sacred cause of Peace is in your hands. In the expectation of a prompt reply . . .

For the first time in his life Peppone disobeyed a Party order. He did not burn the letter. "This is the most eloquent testimonial I have ever received from the Party," he said to himself; "I can't part with an historical document of this kind. If some fool should ever question my merits I'll wave this in his face and send him to the mat. There's nothing more powerful than the printed word."

He read the letter over any number of times, and when he knew it by heart he added: "I've worked hard, all right, but this is a great reward!" His only regret was that he could not show the letter around. "Now," he said, "I must write an answer in equally historic terms, an answer that will bring tears to their eyes. I'll show them what kind of feelings I have in my heart, even if I never went past the third grade in school." That evening he sat down in the cellar to work over his reply.

Comrade:
    I overflow with pride to be chosen for the Peace Brigade and awate further Party orders. Let me anser with the Socialist cry, "I obey!" like the red-shirt Garibaldi, even

:[78]:

if my first impulze is to go rite away. I never asked a favor befor, but now I ask to be alowed to be the first to go.

Peppone read this over and saw that it needed a bit of polish and punctuation. But for a first draft it would do very well. There would be time enough to make a second draft the next day. No need to hurry. It was more important to write the kind of a letter that would be published in the Party papers with a note from the editor above it. And he calculated that three drafts would do the job.

As Don Camillo was smoking his cigar and admiring the beauties of Spring, one evening along the road that led to the mill, he found Peppone in his path. They talked about the time of day and the weather, but it was obvious that there was something Peppone wanted to get off his chest and finally he came out with it.

"Look here, I'd like to talk to you for a minute as man to man instead of as man to priest."

Don Camillo stopped and looked at him hard.

"You're getting off to a poor start," he observed, "by talking like a donkey!"

Peppone made an impatient gesture.

"Don't let's talk politics," he said. "I'd like you to tell me, as man to man, what you think of Russia."

"I've told you that eighty thousand times," said Don Camillo.

"We're quite alone, and no one can overhear us," Peppone insisted. "For once you can be sincere and leave political propaganda out of it. What's it like in Russia, anyhow?"

Don Camillo shrugged his shoulders.

"How should I know, Peppone?" he said. "I've never been there. All I know is what I've read about it. In order to tell you anything more, I'd have to go see for myself. But you ought to know better than I."

"Of course I do," Peppone retorted. "Everyone's well fixed in Russia; everyone has a job. The government is run by the people, and there's no exploitation of the poor. Anything the reactionaries say to the contrary is a lie."

Don Camillo looked at him sharply.

"If you know all that, why do you ask me about it?"

"Just to get your man-to-man opinion. So far I've always heard you talk strictly as a priest."

"And I've always heard you talk as a *comrade*. May I hear your man-to-man opinion as well?"

"To be a comrade means to be a man. And I think as a man just the same way that I think as a comrade."

They walked on for a while, and then Peppone returned to the attack.

"In short, you'd say a fellow's just about as well off in Russia as he is here."

"I said nothing of the sort, but since you say it, I'll admit that's more or less my opinion. Except, of course, for the religious angle."

Peppone nodded.

"We agree then," he said. "But why do you suppose people speak and write so much against it?"

Don Camillo threw out his arms. "Politics . . ."

"Politics! . . . Politics! . . ." muttered Peppone. "America is all mixed up with politics the same way. But no one talks about America quite so violently as about Russia."

"Well, the fact is that people can go see America for themselves, while very few of them have ever set foot in Russia."

Peppone explained that Russia had to be careful. Then he grasped Don Camillo's sleeve and stopped him.

"Listen . . . as man to man, of course. If a fellow had a chance to take a good job in Russia, what would you advise him to do?"

"Peppone, you're asking me quite a tough . . ."

"Man to man, Father . . . I'm sure you have the courage to be frank."

Don Camillo shook his head.

"To be frank, then, I'll say that if it were a question of taking a good job I might advise him to go."

Life is a queer sort of proposition. Logically, Peppone ought to have leaped into the air with joy. But Don Camillo's reply did not make him at all happy. He touched his hat and started to go away. After he had taken a few steps he turned around.

"How can you conscientiously advise a fellow to go to a place where you've never been yourself?" he asked.

"I know more about it than you think," Don Camillo said. "You may not realize it, but I read your newspapers. And some of the people that write for them have been to Russia."

Peppone wheeled abruptly around.

"Oh, the newspapers! . . ." he grunted as he walked away.

Don Camillo was jubilant and he hurried back to the church to tell Christ the whole story.

"Lord, he's got himself into a real mess! He'd like to say he won't go, but in view of his position he doesn't dare turn down the honor. And he came to me in the hope that I'd bolster up his resistance. Now he's caught worse than ever and doesn't see how he can get out of it. I shouldn't like to be in his shoes, I can tell you!"

"And I shouldn't like to be in yours, that is, if God would allow it," Christ answered. "For they're the shoes of a wicked man."

Don Camillo's mouth dropped open.

"I played a good joke on him, that's all," he stammeringly protested.

"A joke's a joke only so long as it doesn't include joy over the victim's pain," Christ enjoined him.

:[81]:

Don Camillo hung his head and left the church. Two days later Peppone received another letter.

Dear Comrade:
   We are sorry to say that, on account of unexpected complications, neither you nor any of the others chosen as members of the Peace Brigade will be able to go to the Soviet Union at this time. Forgive us for causing you this disappointment, but for the moment you can best serve the cause of Peace by staying where you are.

No one ever knew who it was that brought an enormous candle into the church under the cover of darkness that evening. But Don Camillo found it burning near the crucifix when he went that night to say his prayers.

THE STRIKE

Don CAMILLO WALKED
into Peppone's workshop and found the owner sitting in a
corner, reading his paper.

"Labor ennobles man," Don Camillo observed. "Take
care not to overdo it."

Peppone raised his eyes, turned his head to one side in
order to spit, and went on with his reading. Don Camillo
sat down on a box, took off his hat, wiped the perspiration
away from his forehead and remarked calmly: "Good sports-
manship is all that really matters."

Just then Smilzo came in, out of breath from having ridden his racing bicycle so fast. At the sight of Don Camillo, he raised a finger to his cap.

"Greetings, Your Eminence," he said. "The influence exercised by the clergy upon minds still beclouded by the Dark Ages is a brake upon social progress."

Peppone did not stir, and Don Camillo continued to fan himself with his handkerchief, only imperceptibly turning his head so as to look at Smilzo out of the corner of one eye. Smilzo sat down on the floor, leaned up against the wall, and said no more. A few minutes later, Straziami came in with his jacket over one shoulder and his hat pushed back on his head. Taking in the situation at a glance, he stood against the door-post and gazed at the world outside. The next to arrive was Lungo, who pushed some tools to one side of the workbench and sat down on it. Ten minutes went by, and the only sign of life among the five of them was the fanning motion of Don Camillo's hand. Suddenly Peppone crumpled up his paper and threw it away.

"Devil take it!" he exclaimed angrily. "Hasn't anyone got a cigarette?"

Nobody moved, except for Don Camillo, who went on fanning.

"Haven't *you* one?" Peppone asked him maliciously. "I haven't smoked since early this morning."

"And I haven't even smelled tobacco for two whole days," Don Camillo answered. "I was counting on *you*."

Peppone kicked an empty can.

"You asked for it," he shouted. "I hope you're enjoying your De Gasperi government."

"If you were to work instead of reading your paper, you'd have some cigarette money," Don Camillo said calmly.

Peppone threw his cap on the ground.

"Work! Work!" he shouted. "How can I work if no one

brings me anything to do? Instead of having their mowers repaired, people are cutting their hay with a scythe. And my truck hasn't been called out for two months. How am I supposed to get along?"

"Nationalize your business," Don Camillo said calmly.

Smilzo raised a finger.

"The Marshall Plan is the enemy of the people," he began gravely. "And the proletariat needs social reforms, not just a lot of talk."

Peppone got up and stood with his legs wide apart in front of Don Camillo.

"Stop raising a breeze with that damned handkerchief, will you?" he shouted. "And tell us what that government of your choice is doing about the general strike."

"Don't ask me," said Don Camillo. "I can't fit newspapers into my budget. This last month I haven't read anything but my missal."

Peppone shrugged his shoulders.

"It suits you not to know what's going on," he said. "The fact is that you've betrayed the people."

Don Camillo stopped fanning.

"Do you mean me?" he asked gently.

Peppone scratched his head and went back to sit in his corner with his face buried in his hands. In the half-dark workshop silence once more reigned. Each returned to his thoughts on the general strike which had been called from the national headquarters of the Party. Bulletins had been issued, pamphlets distributed and posters put up to explain what the Party leaders were accomplishing for the people, with the result that in the little world of Don Camillo the people were hungry and life in the village was at a standstill. As the days seemed to grow longer and the tempers shorter, Don Camillo had begun to worry.

"To think that on the other side of the river there are people who might work and choose to strike instead!" Don Camillo exclaimed. "At a time like this, I call that a crime!"

He had diplomatically referred to the neighboring township which was outside Peppone's jurisdiction. It was an important agricultural center and there, as everywhere in the valley, the farmers, unable to get labor, were forced to tighten their belts and watch their harvest rot.

Peppone raised his head.

"The strike is the workers' only weapon," he shouted. "Do you want to take it away? What did we fight for in the Resistance movement?"

"To lose the war faster."

So they began to discuss who should pay for the war, and that argument took quite some time. Then they emptied some cans of gasoline into the tank of Lungo's motorcycle, and Smilzo and Lungo rode away, while Don Camillo returned to the rectory.

At midnight a boat shot silently out over the river. In it were five men in overalls, with grease all over their faces, looking like mechanics of some kind; three of them were fellows with especially broad shoulders. They landed on the opposite bank, quite a way downstream, and after walking a mile through empty fields found a truck waiting to take them to a big commerical farm. They proceeded to clean the stable and then to milk the cows. Although there were only five of them, they worked like a whole battalion. Just as they were finishing up with the cows, someone breathlessly spread the alarm: "The squad!"

The five barely had time to get out of the stable by one door before the squad appeared at another, where cans of milk were lined up, ready for delivery. The squad leader kicked over one of the cans and said: "I'll give you a lesson in making butter!" Then, turning to his followers, he added:

"Some of you take care of the rest of the cans, and the others come with me to give a lesson to the strike-breakers."

He advanced threateningly toward the five, but the iron bars wielded by the three with the broad shoulders did the work of eight, and their two smaller companions were as slippery as eels and gave just as much trouble. Before long the squad retired, licking its wounds. But, three hours later, a veritable army came to reënforce it. The five picked up pitchforks and awaited the attack, while their new enemies stopped some sixty feet away.

"We don't want to hurt you," shouted their leader. "We're after the farmer that went and got you from the city. You go on about your business, and we'll settle accounts with him."

The women of the family began to cry, and the farmer and his two sons were white with fear.

"No, we can't let you do that," mumbled one of the five, and they held their ground, while the others, waving sticks, advanced toward them.

"Look out!" said one of the giants. And he threw the pitchfork in the direction of the advancing enemy, who drew back while the pitchfork went into the vacated ground. Then he ran into the stable and reappeared just in time to face the enemy's regrouped forces with a Tommy gun in his hand.

A Tommy gun is no laughing matter, but what is even more frightening is the face of the man who bears it, which reveals from the start whether he intends to shoot or not. In this instance the bearer's face made it very clear that if the enemy didn't cease and desist, he would mow them down. They made another attempt late at night to beseige the stable, but a volley of shots convinced them to keep their distance. The strike-breakers stayed on the job twelve days, until it was all over, and when they went away they were loaded down with foodstuffs and money.

No one ever knew exactly who the strike-breakers were.

But for some time Peppone, Smilzo, Lungo, and Straziami were very quiet. When Don Camillo discussed the matter at the altar, Christ reproached him for having carried a Tommy gun, but Don Camillo insisted it was Peppone. Finally, however, he threw out his arms and gave in.

"What do you expect, Lord?" he said. "How can I explain it to You? We were so alike that no one could say which one was me and which Peppone. All strike-breakers look the same by night."

And when Christ insisted that the Tommy gun had been carried by broad daylight, Don Camillo only threw out his arms again and said: "There are circumstances that cause a man to lose all notion of time!"

THUNDER

TWO DAYS BEFORE THE opening of the hunting season, Lightning died. He was as old as the hills and had every reason to be sick and tired of playing the part of a hunting dog when he wasn't born one. Don Camillo could do nothing but dig a deep hole beside the acacia tree, toss in the body and heave a deep sigh. For a whole fortnight he was depressed, but finally he got over it, and one morning he found himself out in the fields with a shotgun in his hands. A quail rose out of a near-by meadow, and Don

Camillo shot at him, but the quail flew on as calmly as before. Don Camillo nearly yelled: "You wretched dog!" but he remembered that Lightning wasn't there, and felt depressed all over again. He wandered about the fields, over the river bank and under grape arbors, discharged as many volleys as a machine-gun, but never made a single hit. Who could be lucky without a dog beside him?

With the one cartridge he had left, he aimed at a quail flying low over a hedge. He couldn't have missed, but there was no way to be sure. The quail might have fallen either into the hedge or into the field on the other side. But to search for it would be like looking for a needle in a haystack. Better give the whole thing up. He blew into the barrels of his gun and was looking around to find out where he was and what was the shortest way to go home when a rustle caused him to turn his head. Out of the hedge jumped a dog, holding a hare in his mouth, which he proceeded to drop at Don Camillo's feet.

"Heaven help us!" Don Camillo exclaimed. "I shoot a quail, and this dog brings me a hare!"

He picked the hare up and found that it was soaking wet, and so was the dog. Obviously he had swum across from the opposite side of the river. Don Camillo slipped the hare into his bag and started home, with the dog following. When he reached the rectory, the dog crouched outside the door. Don Camillo had never seen a dog like him. He was a fine animal and seemed to be in the pink of condition. Perhaps he was a dog with a pedigree like that of a count or a marquis, but he had no identification papers on him. He wore a handsome collar, but there was no plate or tag attached to it.

"If he doesn't come from another world but has a rightful owner in this one, surely someone will turn up to look for him," Don Camillo thought to himself. And he let the dog in. That evening before going to bed, he thought about the dog and finally put his conscience at rest by saying to himself:

"I'll mention him in church on Sunday." The next morning, when he got up to go say Mass, he forgot all about the dog until he found him at the church door.

"Stay there and wait for me," Don Camillo shouted.

And the dog curled up in front of the sacristy door, where after Mass he gave the priest an enthusiastic greeting. They breakfasted together, and when the dog saw Don Camillo take his shotgun out of the corner where he had left it and hang it on a nail, he barked, ran to the door, returned to see if Don Camillo was following and, in short, would give him no peace until Don Camillo slung the gun over his shoulder and made for the fields. He was an extraordinary dog, one of the kind that puts a hunter on his mettle and makes him think: "If I miss my aim, *I'm* a dirty dog." Don Camillo concentrated as if he were under examination and showed himself to be a worthy master. On his way home with a bag full of game, he said to himself: "I'll call him Thunder." Now that the dog had done his work he was amusing himself by chasing butterflies in a meadow.

"Thunder!" Don Camillo shouted.

It seemed as if from the far side of the meadow someone had launched a torpedo. The dog streaked along with his belly close to the ground, leaving the long grass parted in his wake. He arrived in front of Don Camillo with six inches of tongue hanging out, ready for orders.

"Good dog!" said Don Camillo, and Thunder danced and barked with such joy that Don Camillo thought: "If he doesn't let up, I'll find myself dancing and barking."

Two days went by, and Satan dogged Don Camillo's heels, whispering to him that he should forget to say anything about the dog in church on Sunday. On the afternoon of the third day, when Don Camillo was on his way home with a bag of game and Thunder frisking ahead of him, he ran into Peppone. Peppone was in a gloomy mood; he had been hunting too, but his bag was empty. Now he looked at Thunder, took a newspaper out of his pocket and opened it.

"That's funny," he said. "Looks just like the dog they're advertising as lost."

Don Camillo took the paper from him and found just what he had hoped not to find. Someone from the city was offering a reward to anyone who found a hunting dog with such and such marks upon him, lost three days before along the river.

"Very well, then," said Don Camillo. "I needn't make any announcement in church. Let me keep this paper. I'll give it back to you later."

"It's really too bad," said Peppone. "Everyone says he's an extraordinary dog. And they must be right, because when you had Lightning you never brought home a haul like that one. If I were in your shoes . . ."

"And if I were in yours . . ." Don Camillo interrupted. "But I happen to be in my own, and as an honest man I must restore the dog to his rightful owner."

When they reached the village Don Camillo sent a telegram to the man in the city. Satan was just working out a new argument to use on Don Camillo, but he was too slow, because he had counted on Don Camillo's sending a letter rather than a telegram. That would have taken fifteen or twenty minutes, time enough for anyone so persuasive as Satan to upset the apple-cart. But a five-word telegram was so quickly despatched that Satan was left with his mouth hanging open. Don Camillo went home with his conscience in good order, but with a feeling of deep depression. And he sighed even more deeply than when he had buried Lightning.

The city slicker arrived the next day in a low-slung sport car. He was vain and unpleasant, as might have been expected from his taste in car bodies.

"Where is my dog?" he asked.

:[92]:

"There's a dog been found that must belong to somebody," said Don Camillo. "But you'll have to prove your ownership."

The man described the dog from stem to stern.

"Is that enough?" he asked. "Or do I have to describe his insides as well?"

"That's enough," said Don Camillo glumly, opening the cellar door.

The dog lay on the floor without moving.

"Thunder!" called the city slicker.

"Is that really his name?" asked Don Camillo.

"Yes."

"That's funny."

Still the dog did not move and the man called again:

"Thunder!"

The dog growled and there was an ugly look in his eyes.

"He doesn't seem to be yours," observed Don Camillo.

The city slicker went and took the dog by the collar in order to drag him up from the cellar. Then he turned the collar inside out, revealing a brass plate with a name on it.

"Just read this, Father. Here are my name and address and telephone number. Appearance to the contrary, the dog is mine."

Then he pointed to the car.

"Get in!" he ordered.

The dog obeyed, with his head hanging low and his tail between his legs, and curled up on the back seat. The city slicker held out a five-thousand lira note.

"Here's for your trouble," he said.

"It's no trouble to restore something lost to its rightful owner," said Don Camillo, proudly pushing the money away.

"I'm truly grateful," said the city slicker. "He's a very expensive dog, a thoroughbred from one of the best English kennels, with three international blue ribbons to his credit.

I'm an impulsive sort of fellow, and the other day, when he caused me to miss a hare I gave him a kick. And he resented it."

"He's a dog with professional dignity," said Don Camillo. "And you didn't miss the hare, because he brought it to me."

"Oh well, he'll get over it," said the city slicker, climbing back into his car.

Don Camillo spent a restless night, and when he got up to say Mass the next morning he was immersed in gloom. It was windy and pouring rain, but Thunder was there. He was covered with mud and soaked like a sponge, but he lay in front of the sacristy door and gave Don Camillo a welcome worthy of the last act of an opera. Don Camillo went in and spoke to Christ.

"Lord, Your enemies are going to say that Christians are afraid of wind and water, because not a single one of them has come to church this morning. But if You let Thunder in, they'll be confounded."

Thunder was admitted to the sacristy, where he waited patiently, except when he stuck his nose through the door near the altar, causing Don Camillo to stumble over his prayers. They went back to the rectory together, and the priest sank into his former melancholy.

"No use fooling myself," he said with a sigh. "He knows the way, and he'll come back for you."

The dog growled as if he had understood. He let Don Camillo brush him off and then sat down by the fire to dry. The city slicker returned in the afternoon. He was in a very bad humor, because he had got his car muddy. There was no need of explanations; he walked into the rectory and found Thunder in front of the spent fire.

"Sorry to have given you more trouble," he said, "but it won't happen again. I'll take him to a place of mine in the next province, and he couldn't find his way back from there even if he were a carrier pigeon."

When his master called this time, Thunder gave an angry bark. He would not get into the car of his own accord, but had to be lifted onto the seat. He tried to escape, and when the door was closed he scratched and barked without ceasing.

The next morning Don Camillo left the rectory with his heart pounding. Thunder was not there either that day or the next, and little by little the priest resigned himself to his absence. A fortnight went by, and on the fifteenth night, at about one o'clock, Don Camillo heard a cry from below and knew that it was Thunder. He ran downstairs and out on the church square, quite forgetting that he was in his nightshirt. Thunder was in a very bad condition: starved, dirty, and so tired that he could not hold up his tail. It took three days to restore him to normal, but on the fourth day, after Mass, Thunder pulled him by his cassock over to where the shotgun was hanging and put on such a scene that Don Camillo took his gun, bag, and cartridge belt and set out for the fields. There followed a most unusual week, when Don Camillo's catches made the most seasoned hunters green with envy. Every now and then someone came to see the dog, and Don Camillo explained:

"He's not mine. A man from the city left him here to be trained to chase hares."

One fine morning Peppone came to admire him. He stared at him for some time in silence.

"I'm not going to hunt this morning," said Don Camillo. "Do you want to try him?"

"Will he come?" said Peppone incredulously.

"I think he will. After all, he doesn't know you're a Communist. Seeing you in my company, he probably takes you for a perfectly respectable person."

:[95]:

Peppone was so absorbed by the prospect of trying the dog that he did not answer. Don Camillo turned his gun and bag and cartridge belt over to Peppone. Thunder had been excited to see Don Camillo take down his gun, but now he seemed taken aback.

"Go along with the mayor," said Don Camillo. "I'm busy today."

Peppone put on the belt and hung the gun and bag over his shoulder. Thunder looked at first one man and then the other.

"Go on," Don Camillo encouraged him. "He's ugly, but he doesn't bite."

Thunder started to follow Peppone, but then he stopped in perplexed fashion and turned around.

"Go, go," Don Camillo repeated. "Only watch out that he doesn't enlist you in the Party."

Thunder went along. If Don Camillo had turned over his hunting equipment to this man, he must be a friend. Two hours later he bounded back into the rectory and laid a magnificent hare at Don Camillo's feet. Soon, panting like a locomotive, Peppone arrived upon the scene.

"Devil take you and your dog!" he exclaimed. "He's a perfect wonder, but he eats the game. He stole a hare a yard long. After he had brought me the quails and the partridges, he had to steal a hare."

Don Camillo picked up the hare and held it out to Peppone.

"He's a thinking dog," he answered. "He thought that if the gun and the cartridges were mine, I was entitled to part of the kill."

It was plain that Thunder had acted in good faith, because he did not run away from Peppone but greeted him with affection.

"He's an extraordinary animal," said Peppone, "and I

wouldn't give him back to that man even if he came with a regiment of militia."

Don Camillo sighed.

The city slicker turned up a week later. He wore a hunting outfit and carried a feather-weight Belgian shotgun.

"Well, he got away from up there, too. I've come to see whether he landed here again."

"He arrived yesterday morning," said Don Camillo glumly. "Take him away."

Thunder looked at his master and growled.

"I'll settle accounts with you this time," said the city slicker to the dog.

Thunder growled again, and the city slicker lost his head and gave him a kick.

"You cur! I'll teach you! Lie down!"

The dog lay down, growling, and Don Camillo stepped in.

"He's a thoroughbred, and you can't handle him with violence. Let him quiet down, while you drink a glass of wine."

The man took a seat, while Don Camillo went down to get a bottle from the cellar. While he was there he found time to scribble a note which he gave to the bell-ringer's son.

"Take it to Peppone at his workshop, and hurry."

The note contained only a few words: *The fellow's here again. Lend me twenty thousand liras so I can try to buy the dog. And get them here fast.*

The city slicker drank several glasses of wine, talked idly to Don Camillo, then looked at his watch and stood up.

"I'm sorry, but I must go. Friends are expecting me for the hunt, and I've just time to get there."

Thunder was still crouching in a corner and as soon as he saw his master he started growling. He growled louder when the man came near. Just then there came the roar of a motorcycle and Don Camillo saw Peppone dismount from it. He made an interrogative gesture and Peppone nodded an affirmative answer. He held up two open hands, then one, and finally one finger. Then with his right hand he made a horizontal cut through the air. Which signified that he had sixteen thousand five hundred liras. Don Camillo sighed with relief.

"Sir," he said to the city slicker. "You can see that the dog has taken a dislike to you. Thoroughbreds don't forget, and you'll never make him put it behind him. Why don't you sell him to me?"

Then he made a mental calculation of all his resources and added.

"I can pay you eighteen thousand eight hundred liras. That's all I possess."

The city slicker sneered.

"Father, you must be joking. The dog cost me eighty thousand and I wouldn't sell him for a hundred. He may have taken a dislike to me, but I'll make him get over it."

Heedless of Thunder's growling, he seized him by the collar and dragged him over to the car. As he tried to lift him in, the struggling dog clawed some paint off the fender. The city slicker lost his head and with his free hand beat him over the back. The dog continued to struggle, caught the hand that was holding his collar and bit it. The city slicker let go, and the dog went to lie against the rectory wall, still growling. Don Camillo and Peppone stood staring and did not have time to say a word. The city slicker, as pale as a corpse, pulled his shotgun out of the car and aimed it at the animal.

"You bastard!" he said between his teeth, as he shot it off.

The wall of the rectory was stained with blood, and after a piercing howl, Thunder lay motionless on the ground. The city slicker got into his car and drove off at top speed. Don Camillo did not notice his departure or the fact that Peppone had followed him on his motorcycle. He knelt beside the dog, with all his attention fixed upon him. The dog groaned as Don Camillo stroked his head, and then suddenly licked his hand. Then he got up and barked happily.

After twenty minutes, Peppone returned. He was red in the face and his fists were clenched.

"I caught up with him at Fiumaccio, where he had to stop at the grade crossing. I dragged him out of the car and boxed his ears until his head was as big as a watermelon. He reached for his gun, and I broke it over his back."

They were in the hall, and now a howl came from farther inside.

"Isn't he dead yet?" asked Peppone.

"Only his flanks were grazed," said Don Camillo. "In a week he'll be livelier than ever."

Peppone ran a big hand dubiously over his chin.

"Morally speaking," said Don Camillo, "he killed the dog. When he shot that was his intention. If Saint Anthony deflected his aim, that doesn't take away from the vileness of the deed. You were wrong to box his ears, because violence is never a good thing. But in any case . . ."

"In any case . . . He won't show his face here again," said Peppone, "and you have acquired a dog."

"Half a dog," specified Don Camillo. "Because I'm morally indebted to you for the money you were ready to lend me. So half the dog is yours."

Peppone scratched his head.

"What do you know about that!" he exclaimed. "An honest priest, and one that doesn't defraud the people!"

Don Camillo gave him a threatening look.

"Listen, if you bring politics into it, I'll change my mind and keep the dog to myself!"

"Consider it unsaid!" exclaimed Peppone, who underneath it all was a man and a hunter and cared more for Thunder's

:[99]:

esteem than for that of Marx, Lenin and company. And Thunder, with a bandage around his hips, came barking in to seal the pact of non-aggression.

PEOPLE CALLED IT Manasca's Garden, but it was just a quarter of an acre of underbrush, with weeds as tall as poplars, surrounded by a ten-foot wall. A forgotten plot with a hundred and fifty feet of frontage on the square and ninety feet on the tree-lined street leading into it. Because it was the only vacant lot on the square, old Manasca had been offered any amount of money for it, but he had never been willing to sell. For years and years it lay there, just as fallow and uncultivated as its owner, until finally the old man died and it was inherited by his son, together with a pile of thousand-lira notes and other pieces of property here and there on both sides of the river. Young Manasca thought it was a shame not to put the plot to use and finally he went to see the mayor.

"Men are starving because they can't find work," he said very directly, "but you proletarians, as you call yourselves, with all your red kerchiefs, are such a filthy bunch that it's a sin to give you anything to do."

"We're not as filthy as you fine gentlemen," Peppone answered peacefully. "The best of you deserves to be strung up on a rope made of the guts of the most miserable of us."

Young Manasca and Peppone had had a fist-fight every day until they were twenty; as a result they were very good friends and understood one another perfectly. So now Peppone asked what he was driving at.

"If you promise you won't trip me up with trade-unions, Party, vice-Party, victims of the Resistance movement, social justice, rightful claims, sympathy strikes and all the rest of your revolutionary paraphernalia, I'll provide work for half the men in the village," Manasca told him.

Peppone put his fists on his hips.

"Do you want me to help you exploit the worker? To convince him he ought to work for a dish of cornmeal mush and a kick in the pants?"

"I don't intend to cheat anybody. I'll pay regular wages and old-age insurance and give you a barrel of wine in the bargain if you promise me that those stupid fools won't walk out in the middle of the job and try to blackmail me. It's a big project, and if it doesn't come off, I'm a ruined man."

Peppone told him to lay his cards on the table.

"I propose to throw up a five-storey building in the garden," said Manasca. "Big-city stuff, with a hundred-foot arcade on the square, shops, a café, a restaurant with rooms to rent above it, a garage, a gasoline pump and so on. If all goes well, I'll let you run the gasoline pump. However much of nuisance you are, you know how to make things go. With a building like that we'll make this into an important market center and turn our yokels into sophisticates."

Peppone had never laid eyes on Paris or London or New York, but he imagined the new building as on the order of theirs. And he could see a red-and-yellow gasoline pump in front of his workshop, with a pump for compressed air as well.

"A complete filling-station needs a hydraulic machine to lift cars up for greasing," he murmured.

"There'll be a hydraulic machine and all the other gadgets you can think of," said Manasca. "But you've got to make me a promise."

"What if I'm not re-elected mayor?" Peppone said, worriedly.

"So much the better! The new mayor will be afraid of you and your gang. And that's more than you can say for yourself!"

Peppone brought a fist down on his desk.

"That's a bargain! And I'll kill the first man that gives you trouble. The future of the village is concerned, and anyone that doesn't do a good job will get a swift kick. Tell me what you need and I'll find you the right people."

"Let's have a clear understanding," said Manasca. "You're not to hire only people from your own party. I want men that are willing to work and have the know-how."

"That's right; all men are equal when they're hungry," Peppone said sententiously.

And that very evening, with due solemnity he gave the news to his party stalwarts.

"Tell people that while others chatter, we actually do something. We're building a skyscraper."

A week later, a crew of wreckers began to tear down the wall. And then it was that trouble began. The wall was a mass of stones and rubble and mortar, at least three hundred years old, which was easy enough to smash, but there was something on the wall that everyone had forgotten. On the street side, just a yard before the corner, there was a niche, with a rusty grating over it to protect a Madonna painted inside.

The Madonna was a thing of no artistic value, painted by some poor devil two or three hundred years before, but everyone knew her; everyone had greeted her a thousand times and stopped to put a flower in the tin can at her feet. And if the wall around her was torn down, the Madonna would fall to pieces. Manasca sent for an expert from the city, one of those fellows who can peel a painting off a wall. But after studying the situation he declared that there was nothing to do.

"If we so much as touch the painting, it will crumble into dust."

Meanwhile the wreckers were advancing, and when they were a couple of yards away on either side, they stopped. Peppone came to look at the Madonna clinging to the last bit of wall and shook his head.

"Nonsense!" he said. "This isn't religion; it's superstition. There's no intention of hurting anybody's feelings. For the sake of this painting are we to give up a plan that's providing work for a lot of people and doing something for the village as well?"

The wreckers were tough fellows, who would just as soon have demolished their own mothers. But there they stood in front of the remaining scrap of wall. Their chief, Bago, spat out a cigarette butt and shook his head.

"I wouldn't destroy it even on orders from the Pope!" he exclaimed, and the others looked as if they felt about the same way.

"No one said anything about destroying it," shouted Peppone. "That's all sentimentality, traditionalism, childishness and so on. There's only one thing to do, to tear down as much of the wall as possible, then to prop up and protect what's left, lift it away and put it somewhere else. In Russia they move fifteen-storey buildings from one street to another, and no matter how far we may be behind them, we ought to be able to pull off a trick like this one."

Bago shrugged his shoulders.

"In Russia they may move buildings, but they haven't **any** Madonnas to move," he mumbled.

Brusco took a good look and then threw out his arms in despair.

"There's a crack at the back of the niche, and it's a miracle that the whole thing didn't fall apart years ago. The wall's made of mud and stones, and if you try to lift a piece of it out you'll be left with a fistful of sand."

Peppone strode up and down, and half the village gathered to look on.

"Well then, what have you got to say, all of you?" Peppone snarled. "You can see the situation for yourselves. Are we to stop work or not? Say something, or may God strike you dead!"

But no one seemed to have any answer.

"We'd better go see the priest about it," was their conclusion.

Peppone jammed his cap down on his head.

"All right. Since the future of the village is at stake, I suppose we'll have to call upon the priest."

Don Camillo was transplanting some vegetables in his garden when Peppone and the rest of them looked over the hedge. Manasca explained the problem, and Peppone put the question:

"What shall we do?"

Don Camillo asked for further details and prolonged the discussion. Of course, he already knew what it was all about and only wanted to gain time.

"It's late now," he said at last. "We'll decide tomorrow."

"In the city I've seen any number of churches that have been de-consecrated and taken over by coal merchants or cabinet-makers," said Peppone. "If a church can be transformed that way, why can't we do the same thing with a picture painted on a wall?"

"The very fact that you've come to consult me shows that there are some difficulties in your minds," said Don Camillo.

That night the priest could not sleep for worry. But the next morning, when Peppone and his gang appeared before him, he had a solution.

"If you are quite sure in your consciences that there is no way of saving the picture, then go ahead and tear down the wall. It's for the good of the whole community, and a poor old painted Madonna wouldn't want to take bread out of men's mouths and stand in the way of progress. God be with you! But go at it gently."

"Very well," said Peppone, touching his cap, and marching off with his men to the square.

When they reached the Madonna he turned and said to Bago:

"You heard what the priest told us, didn't you? We're not giving offense to anyone."

Bago twisted the visor of his cap to one side of his head, spit into his hands and grasped the handle of his pick. He raised the pick in the air, left it suspended there for several minutes, and then said: "Not me! I'll not be the one to do it."

Peppone stormed and shouted, but none of the men was willing to deliver the fatal blow. Finally he seized the pick himself and advanced toward the wall. He raised it above

:[106]:

his head, but when through the grating he saw the Madonna's eyes upon him, he threw it down on the ground.

"Devil take it!" he exclaimed. "Why should this be the mayor's job? What has a mayor to do with the Madonna? The priest ought to be good for something. Let him do it! Everyone to his own trade, I say."

And he went angrily back to the rectory.

"All done?" Don Camillo asked him.

"The devil it's done!" shouted Peppone. "It's no use."

"Why?"

"Because the Madonna and saints are your racket. I've never called on you to smash a bust of Marx or Lenin, have I?"

"No, but if you want me to, I'd be glad to oblige," said Don Camillo.

Peppone clenched his fists.

"Do what you see fit," said Peppone. "But remember that as long as the Madonna's there, we can't go on with the work, and you'll be responsible for the resulting unemployment. I'm a mayor by profession, not a destroyer of Madonnas. And I don't want to be told that we're a bunch of sacrilegious Reds, smashing up saints wherever we find them."

"Very well, then," said Don Camillo. "The rest of you can go along, while I talk to the mayor."

When the two men were left alone together, they said nothing for several minutes. Then Don Camillo broke the silence.

"Peppone, it's no good, I can't tear it down."

"Neither can I," said Peppone. "If you, who specialize in saints, haven't got the nerve . . ."

"It's not a question of nerve," said Don Camillo. "It's the way it was with the angel in the bell tower, that for hundreds of years had looked down on the village. The eyes of this Madonna have seen all our beloved dead, they have reflected the hope and despair, the joys and sorrows of centuries past. Do you remember, Peppone, when we came back from the war in 1918? I gave the Madonna flowers, and you gave your tin cup to put them in."

Peppone grunted, and Don Camillo ran his hand over his chin. Then he threw his coat around him and put on his hat. When they arrived in front of the Madonna, they found half the village waiting there. There was a stranger also, a young man who had come in a car, and from the manner in which Peppone ran to greet him, it was clear that he was a Party bigwig from the city. Now he stepped forward and looked at the Madonna.

"Well," he said, "if things are the way you tell me and the priest agrees that you can't give up a project that's so beneficial to the community and to the working-man, then I'll be the one to cut through your middle-class sentimentality. I'll do the job myself."

He took a pick and started over to the wall. But Don Camillo laid a hand on his shoulder and pulled him back.

"It's not necessary," he said roughly.

There was a deep silence, while everyone looked expectantly at the wall. Suddenly the wall quivered and then slowly cracked open. The wall did not fall to the ground, it crumbled into a heap of stones and plaster. On top of the heap, free of the rusty grating and the shadows of the niche in which it had dwelt for so long, stood the Madonna, completely unscathed. Although she had been painted two or three hundred years before, she was as fresh as a rose.

"She can go back to the same place in the new wall," said Manasco.

"Motion carried by unanimous applause!" shouted Peppone. And he thought of his old army tin cup, with the offering of flowers from Don Camillo.

:[108]:

ONE AFTERNOON AN OLD woman by the name of Maria Barchini came to confession. Don Camillo listened to her quietly, but toward the end he was startled almost out of his skin to hear her say hesitantly: "Father, I'm going to vote for the Communists."

He came out of the confessional and said to her: "Come along over to the rectory." And when they had sat down in his study, he asked if there were anything wrong with her head.

"I thought I'd explained all these things any number of times," he told her. "Didn't you understand me?"

"Yes, I understood," said the old woman. "I'm willing to do whatever penance you prescribe, to fast or make a pilgrimage to the Sanctuary . . . But I'm voting for the Communists."

"There's no use in my wasting breath to explain something you say you already understand," Don Camillo said brusquely. "If you vote for those people, I can't give you absolution."

She spread out her arms in a gesture of resignation.

"God will forgive me," she said, "and I'll pay whatever the price may be. The main thing is for my boy to come home. A mother must be ready to sacrifice herself for her son."

Don Camillo looked at her in bewilderment and asked her what her son had to do with the election.

"Two ladies came from the city the other day," she explained, "and promised that if I voted for the right candidates my boy would be sent back from Russia. These people are friendly to the Russians, and if they win they'll bring back the prisoners of war. They took down my name and put it high on their list. And I gave them the boy's picture. I can understand why you can't give me absolution, but I still say a mother must sacrifice herself for her child."

Don Camillo shook his head.

"I see," he muttered. "But you've got to be sure your boy will really come."

"I had lost all hope until they gave it back to me. When you're drowning, you know, you'll clutch at any straw."

"I see," said Don Camillo. "But what if the Communists don't win?"

"Ah well . . ." the old woman sighed. "I have to do all I

can. They put his name at the head of the list. I saw them write it down. And they were respectable people, educated people. They said they knew the way things are, but a mother has to do everything she can for her son. I'll have to vote for the 'People's Front.' "

Don Camillo stood up and traced a cross in the air.

"*Ego te absolvo*," he said. "Say four Our Fathers, four Hail Marys and four Glorias for penance. And God be praised."

And when from his window he saw the old woman leave the church, he went to talk to Christ on the altar.

"Lord," Don Camillo said impetuously, "if a woman is willing to sacrifice herself in the hope of saving her son, Don Camillo has no right to take her hope away. If I had refused her absolution it would have been like saying: 'You're willing to make any sacrifice for your boy, but God is against you.' And that would have been a wicked thing to say, for even when hope is based on material things, its origin is divine. In Your divine wisdom You know how to turn evil means to a good end, and You chose to speak through sacrilegious mouths in order to restore hope to a mother's heart. To refuse her absolution would have meant telling her she had no right to hope, and to deny hope means to deny You."

Christ smiled.

"What are you driving at, Don Camillo?" he asked. "Do you want me to vote for the 'People's Front'?"

"I merely wanted to explain why I gave old Maria Barchini absolution in spite of the fact that she's voting for the Communists."

"And why must you explain, Don Camillo? Did I ask for any explanation? Aren't you at peace with your own conscience?"

"I'm not, Lord, that's just the trouble. I should have taken away from Your enemies the vote they have extorted from that poor woman."

"But her illusions have been turned into hope, and you have just said that hope is divine, Don Camillo."

Don Camillo ran his big hands over his face.

"That's equally true," he admitted. "What's to be done?"

"I can't tell you," Christ said with a smile. "I don't go in for politics."

Peppone was in his workshop, busy repainting a fender of his truck, when Don Camillo accosted him.

"Some of your filthy propagandists are going around telling poor people whose boys are still in Russia that if they vote for the Communists the Russians will send all the prisoners home."

"I don't believe it," muttered Peppone. "Give me the names of some of the people."

"That would be violating the secrecy of the confessional. But I swear to you it's true."

Peppone shrugged his shoulders.

"I didn't send anybody out on such a mission. It must be an idea from the city. Anyhow, we're at war, aren't we? And each side must use whatever cards he has in his hand."

"Exactly," said Don Camillo gloomily.

"You have a trick up your sleeve, for that matter. If someone votes for us, you won't grant him absolution."

"I shan't refuse absolution to anyone who's been given the false hope of recovering a son. But when the time comes, God will refuse absolution to you. You're damning your own soul!"

Don Camillo spoke very calmly and then went away. Peppone stared after him, open-mouthed, for he had never heard

Don Camillo speak just this way before, in a cold, far-away voice that seemed to come from another world. He thought of it several times both that day and the next. Then posters appeared on the walls announcing a meeting of the Socialist Unity Party and, in accordance with directives from headquarters, he had to organize a counter-demonstration. On Sunday the village was packed with people.

"In the front row, just below the platform, put the comrades from Molinetto and Torricella," ordered Peppone. "At the first slip made by one of the Socialist speakers they're to go into action. Our own people are all going to Molinetto and Torricella to do the same job at the Christian Democrat and Nationalist rallies. Brusco and I and the rest of the local leaders will stay in the Town Hall. We're not to appear on the scene unless there's trouble."

The Socialist speaker was about thirty-five years old, a well-bred man and a born orator. As soon as Peppone heard the voice he jumped up on a chair and peered out the window.

"It's him!" he stammered. And Brusco and Bigio and Smilzo and all the rest agreed that it was him indeed, and had nothing more to say.

A few minutes later, the nuisance squad went into action. The speaker made telling answers to their insults and accusations, and finally they lost control of themselves and made a rush for the platform. Peppone signaled to them from the window, but it was too late. The crowd gathered in front of the house where the speaker had been rushed to safety. Peppone and his seconds made their way through to the door. The speaker was sitting on a sofa inside, while a woman bandaged his hand. He had blood on his face because someone had struck him with a key across the forehead. Peppone looked at him, gaping.

"Hello there, Peppone," said the wounded man, raising his head. "Did you organize this little party?"

Peppone did not answer, and the wounded man smiled again.

"Ah, so Brusco's here, and Smilzo, and Straziami, and Lungo. Well, I'm here too. Our old group is together again, all except for Rosso and Giacomino, who died in our mountain encampment. Who could have imagined that Peppone was going to organize a party like this for his old commander? . . ."

Peppone spread out his arms.

"Chief, I didn't know . . ." he stammered.

"Oh, don't let that bother you," the wounded man interrupted him. "We're at war, and everyone plays the cards he can. I quite see your point of view." The bandage was finished, and he got up to go. "So long, Comrade Peppone," he said with a smile. "We saved our skins from the Germans; now let's hope we can save them from the Communists, too. Rosso and Giacomino are lucky to have died when they did, up in the mountains."

He got into a waiting car, and Peppone heard the hooting and shouting that accompanied its departure. When the "chief" had spoken that last sentence, his voice had been as cold and far-away and other-worldly as Don Camillo's when he had said: "You're damning your own soul!"

That evening, the leaders of the squads that had done a job at Molinetto and Torricella came to report. At Molinetto the Christian Democrat speaker had been forced to stop halfway through his address, and nothing serious had happened. At Torricella the Nationalist had received a slap in the face. Peppone knew them both. The first was a university professor and the second had been in a German labor camp.

"They gave them an even rougher time in the city," the leader of the Molinetto squad was saying. "They trampled down some students and gave a police sergeant a black eye."

"Good," said Peppone, getting up to leave the room.

:[114]:

The sun was setting as he walked slowly along the road leading down to the river. On the bank someone was smoking a cigar and looking into the water. It was Don Camillo. They said nothing for a while, until Peppone observed that it was a fine evening.

"Very fine," Don Camillo answered.

Peppone lit the butt of a cigar, inhaled a few mouthfuls of smoke, then put it out with his shoe. He spat angrily.

"Everybody's against us," he said glumly. "Even my old Partisan commander. Everybody, including God."

Don Camillo went on quietly smoking. "Everybody's not against you. You're against everybody, God included."

Peppone crossed his arms on his chest. "Why did you say I was damning my own soul? Just because old Maria Barchini's going to give us her vote?"

"Maria Barchini? Who's she?"

"I went around yesterday to see all the families whose boys are prisoners in Russia, and she told me that two women had called upon her on behalf of the People's Front. I told her that they were fakers and that even if she were to vote as they said she'd never see her son again."

Don Camillo threw away his cigar.

"And what did she say?"

"She asked how she was to vote in order to get back her son. I told her I didn't know, and she said if no party could bring him back then there was no use voting at all."

"You're an idiot," said Don Camillo.

He said it solemnly, but not in that cold far-away voice. Peppone felt better. When he thought of the blood on his former commander's face and the slap given to the former labor-camp inmate at Molinetto and the old professor at Torricella who couldn't finish his address because of the shouting, he felt like crying. But he took hold of himself and shouted fiercely:

"We're going to win!"

"No," Don Camillo said calmly but firmly.

For a moment they just stood there silently, each one looking straight ahead. The valley stretched out peacefully under the evening sky and the river was just the same as it had been a hundred thousand years before. And so was the sun. It was about to set, but the next morning it would rise again from the opposite direction. Peppone—who can say why?—found himself thinking of this extraordinary fact and privately came to the conclusion that, to tell the truth, God knows his business.

TECHNIQUE OF THE
COUP D'ETAT

AT TEN O'CLOCK ON TUES-
day evening the village square was swept with wind and rain,
but a crowd had been gathered there for three or four hours
to listen to the election news coming out of a radio loud-
speaker. Suddenly the lights went out and everything was
plunged into darkness. Someone went to the control box but
came back saying there was nothing to be done. The trouble
must be up the line or at the power plant, miles away. People
hung around for a half hour or so, and then, as the rain began

to come down even harder than before, they scattered to their homes, leaving the village silent and deserted. Peppone shut himself up in the People's Palace, along with Lungo, Brusco, Straziami and Gigio, the lame leader of the "Red Wing" squad from Molinetto. They sat around uneasily by the light of a candle stump and cursed the power and light monopoly as an enemy of the people, until Smilzo burst in. He had gone to Roccaverde on his motorcycle to see if anyone had news and now his eyes were popping out of his head and he was waving a sheet of paper.

"The Front has won!" he panted. "Fifty-two seats out of a hundred in the Senate and fifty-one in the Chamber. The other side is all washed up. We must get hold of our people and have a celebration. If there's no light, we can set fire to a couple of haystacks near by."

"Hurrah!" shouted Peppone. But Gigio grabbed hold of Smilzo's jacket.

"Shut your trap and stay where you are!" he said grimly. "It's too early for anyone to be told. Let's take care of our little list."

"List? What list?" asked Peppone in astonishment.

"The list of reactionaries who are to be bumped off first thing. Let's see now . . ."

Peppone stammered that he had made no such list, but the other only laughed.

"That doesn't matter. I've a very complete one here all ready. Let's look at it together, and once we've decided, we can get to work."

Gigio pulled a sheet of paper with some twenty names on it out of his pocket and laid it on the table.

"Looks to me as if all the reactionary pigs were here," he said. "I put down the worst of them, and we can attend to the rest later."

Peppone scanned the names and scratched his head.

"Well, what do you say?" Gigio asked him.

"Generally speaking, we agree," said Peppone. "But what's the hurry? We have plenty of time to do things in the proper style."

Gigio brought his fist down on the table.

"We haven't a minute to lose, that's what I say," he shouted harshly. "This is the time to put our hands on them, before they suspect us. If we wait until tomorrow, they may get wind of something and disappear."

At this point Brusco came into the discussion.

"You must be crazy," he said. "You can't go around bumping people off without thinking it over."

"I'm not crazy, and you're a very poor Communist, that's what you are! These are all reactionary pigs; no one can dispute that, and if you don't take advantage of this golden opportunity then you're a traitor to the Party!"

Brusco shook his head.

"Nothing doing! It's jackasses that are traitors to the Party! And you'll make a jackass of yourself if you go around making mistakes and bumping off innocent people."

Gigio raised a threatening finger.

"It's better to eliminate ten innocents than to spare one individual who may be dangerous to the cause. Dead men can do the Party no harm. "You're a very poor Communist, as I've said before. In fact, you never were a good one. You're a weak sister, a softie, I say; you're just a *bourgeois* in disguise!"

Brusco grew pale, and Peppone intervened.

"That's enough," he said. "Comrade Gigio has the right idea, and nobody can deny it. It's part of the groundwork of Communist philosophy. Communism gives us the goal at

:[119]:

which to aim and democratic discussion must be confined to the choice of the quickest and surest ways to attain it."

Gigio nodded his head in satisfaction, while Peppone continued: "Once it's been decided that these persons are or may be dangerous to the cause and therefore we must eliminate them, the next thing is to figure out the best method of elimination. Because if we were by our carelessness to allow a single reactionary to escape, then we should indeed be traitors to the Party. Is that clear?"

"Absolutely," the others said in chorus. "You're dead right."

"There are six of us," Peppone went on, "and twenty names on the list, among them Filotti, who has a whole regiment in his house and a cache of arms in the cellar. If we were to attack these people one by one, at the first shot the rest would run away. We must call our forces together, and divide them up into twenty squads, each one equipped to deal with a particular objective."

"Very good," said Gigio.

"Good, my eye!" shouted Peppone. "That's not the half of it! We need a twenty-first squad, equipped even better than the rest, to hold off the police. And mobile squads to cover the roads and the river. If a fellow rushes into action the way you proposed, without proper precautions, running the risk of botching it completely, then he's not a good Communist, he's just a damned fool."

It was Gigio's turn to pale now, and he bit his lip in anger while Peppone proceeded to give orders. Smilzo was to transmit word to the cell leaders in the outlying settlements, and these were to call their men together. A green rocket would give the signal to meet in appointed places, where Falchetto Brusco and Straziami would form the squads and assign the targets. A red rocket would mean to go into action

Smilzo went off on his motorcycle, while Lungo, Brusco, Straziami, and Gigio discussed the make-up of the squads.

"You must do a faultless job," Peppone told them. "I shall hold you personally responsible for its success. Meanwhile I'll see if the police are on the alert and find some way to put them off."

Don Camillo, after waiting in vain for the lights to go on and the radio to resume its mumbling, thinking there would be no more callers that evening, decided to get ready for bed. Suddenly he heard a knock at the door, and when he drew it open cautiously, he found Peppone before him.

"Get out of here in a hurry!" Peppone panted. "Pack a bag and go! Put on an ordinary suit of clothes, take your boat and row down the river."

Don Camillo stared at him with curiosity.

"Comrade Mayor, have you been drinking?"

"Hurry!" said Peppone. "The People's Front has won, and the squads are getting ready. There's a list of people to be bumped off, and your name is the first one!"

Don Camillo bowed.

"An unexpected honor, Mr. Mayor! But I must say I never expected you to be the sort of rascal that goes around making up lists of people to be murdered."

"Don't be silly," said Peppone impatiently. "I don't want to murder anybody."

"Well then?"

"Gigio, the lame fellow from Molinetto, came out with the list and secret Party orders."

"You're the chief, Peppone. You could have sent him and his list to blazes."

Peppone rubbed his perspiring face.

"You don't understand these things. The Party always has

the last word, and he was speaking for the Party. If I'd stood out against him he'd have added my name to the list, above yours."

"That's a good one! Comrade Peppone and the reactionary priest, Don Camillo, strung up together!"

"Hurry, will you?" Peppone repeated. "You can afford to joke because you're all alone in the world, but I have a mother, a wife, a son and a whole lot of other dependents. Move fast if you want to save your skin!"

Don Camillo shook his head.

"Why should I be saved? What about the others?"

"I can't very well go to warn them, can I? You'll have to do that yourself. Drop in on one or two of them on your way to the river, and tell them to pass on the alarm. And they'd better shake a leg! Here, take down the names."

"Very well," said Don Camillo when he'd taken them down. "I'll send the sexton's boy to call the Filotti family, and there are so many of them that they can take care of the rest. I'm staying right here."

"But you've got to go, I tell you!"

"This is my place, and I won't budge, even if Stalin comes in person."

"You're crazy!" said Peppone, but before he could say anything else, there was a knock at the door and he had to run and hide in the next room.

The next arrival was Brusco, but he had barely time to say: "Don Camillo, get out of here in a hurry!" before someone knocked at the door again. Brusco, too, ran to hide, and a minute later Lungo burst in.

"Don Camillo," said Lungo, "I've only just been able to sneak away for a minute. Things are getting hot, and you'd better beat it. Here are the names of the other people you ought to take with you."

And he rushed to hide, because there was another knock a

the door. This time it was Straziami, as glum and pugnacious as ever. He had hardly stepped in, when Lungo, Brusco, and Peppone emerged to meet him.

"It's beginning to look like one of those old-fashioned comedies," said Don Camillo, laughing. "As soon as Gigio comes, the whole cast will be on the stage."

"He's not coming," muttered Peppone.

Then with a sigh, he slapped Brusco on the back.

"What do you know about that?" he said reminiscently. "Here we are again, the way we were up in the mountains in the old days of the Resistance. And we can still get along together."

The others nodded.

"If Smilzo were only here the old guard would be complete," sighed Peppone.

"He *is* here," said Don Camillo. "In fact, he was the first to come."

"Good," said Peppone approvingly. "And now you'd better hustle."

But Don Camillo was a stubborn man.

"I told you once that my place is here," he said. "I'm quite happy enough to know that you're not against me."

Peppone lost patience. He twisted his hat around and then jammed it down on his head the way he did when he was ready to come to blows.

"You two take his shoulders, and I'll take his legs," he ordered. "It's too late to go by boat. We'll tie him to the seat of his cart and send him away. Straziami, go harness the horse."

But before they could raise their arms the lights went on, and they stood there, dazzled. A moment later the radio began to mumble.

"Here are the results of the election of Deputies to Parliament, with 41,000 out of 41,168 electoral districts heard from: Christian Democrats, 12,000,257 votes; People's Front, 7,547,468 . . ."

They all listened in silence until the announcement was over. Then Peppone looked gloomily at Don Camillo.

"Some weeds are so tough that they overrun everything," he said angrily. "You had a lucky escape, that's all I can say."

"You had a lucky escape yourself," Don Camillo answered calmly, "for which God be praised."

One man didn't escape and that was Gigio. He was proudly waiting for orders to set off the green rocket and, instead, he got a volley of kicks that left him black and blue all over.

BENEFIT OF CLERGY

THE TIME HAS COME TO
speak of Smilzo, official messenger at the Town Hall, and head
of the "flying squad" of the local Communist Party, and to
brand him for what he was, an example of flagrant immoral-
ity, or rather a man without any sense of shame. Because a
man must be shameless to live openly with a woman to whom
he is not married in a village of the Po valley. And the woman
who shared his bed and board was just as shameless as he.

People called Moretta a "kept woman," but in reality she
was a girl quite capable of keeping herself. She was big-

boned and as strong as any man, and farmers hired her to run a tractor, which she manoeuvered just as skillfully as Peppone. Although the women of the village referred to her as "that hussy," no man had ever made advances to her without getting a slap in the face that left him groggy. Nevertheless it was a village scandal to see Smilzo carry her on the handlebars of his bicycle, which was where she rode when she didn't occupy the saddle and carry him.

Don Camillo had come into the world with a constitutional preference for calling a spade a spade and so it was that he spoke from the pulpit of "certain women who rode around on racing bicycles, flaunting their flanks as freely as their faces." From then on, Moretta wore blue denims and a red kerchief around her neck, which left the village even more shocked than before. Once Don Camillo managed to catch hold of Smilzo and say something to him about "legalizing the situation," but Smilzo only jeered in his face.

"There's nothing to 'legalize' about it. We do nothing more and nothing less than people who are idiotic enough to get married."

"Than decent men and women . . ." Don Camillo sputtered.

"Than idiots who spoil the beauty of a union between two sister souls by dragging a clumsy oaf of a mayor or a priest reeking of tobacco into it."

Don Camillo swallowed the aspersion on his tobacco and came back to the main point of what he was saying. But Smilzo continued to jeer at him.

"If God Almighty had intended men and women to be joined in matrimony, He'd have put a priest with Adam and Eve in the Garden of Eden! Love was born free and free it ought to remain! The day is coming when people will understand that marriage is like a jail sentence and they'll get along

:[126]:

without benefit of clergy. And when that day comes there'll be dancing in the churches."

Don Camillo found only a brick handy. He picked this up and threw it, but Smilzo had learned during the period of the Resistance movement to slip between one volley of machine-gun fire and another, and so the brick was wasted. But Don Camillo was not discouraged, and one day he lured Moretta to the rectory. She came in her blue denims, with the red kerchief around her neck and lit a cigarette as soon as she sat down before him. Don Camillo refrained from scolding her and spoke in the mildest tone of voice he could manage.

"You're a hard-working girl and a good housekeeper," he told her. "I know that you don't gossip or waste money. And I know too that you love your husband . . ."

"He isn't my husband," Moretta interrupted.

"That you love Smilzo, then," said Don Camillo patiently. "And so, although you've never come to confession, I'm convinced that you're a decent sort of woman. Why do you have to behave in such a way that people brand you as indecent?"

" 'People' can go straight to . . . where they belong," Moretta retorted.

Don Camillo was growing red in the face, but he went ahead with his plan and murmured something about getting married. But Moretta interrupted him.

"If God Almighty had intended men and women to be joined in matrimony. . . ."

"Never mind," said Don Camillo, interrupting her in his turn. "I know the rest already."

"Love was born free and free it ought to remain!" Moretta concluded gravely. "Marriage is the opium of love."

The village gossips did not give up so easily. They formed a committee and went to tell the mayor that the affair was bringing shame upon the village and for the sake of public morals he must do something about it.

"I'm married myself," said Peppone, "and I have a right to perform a civil marriage, but I can't force people to marry when they don't want to. That's the law. Perhaps when the Pope comes into power things will be different."

But the old crones insisted.

"If you can't do anything as mayor, then as head of the local section of the Party you can bring pressure on them. They're a disgrace to the Party, too."

"I'll try," said Peppone, and so he did.

"I'd rather join the *Socialist* Party than marry," was Smilzo's answer.

That was all there was to it, and with the passage of time the scandal abated, or rather politics took its place. But one day it came to the fore again and in a clamorous manner. For some time Comrade Moretta was not seen about, and then all of a sudden there was a startling piece of news. There were no longer two Comrades, but three, because, as the midwife told it, a little girl had been born to them, and one far prettier than they deserved. The old crones of the village began to wag their tongues again, and those who were politically minded said:

"There are Communist morals for you. It's a hundred to one those godless parents will never have the child baptized."

This got around to Peppone, and he rushed to the godless parents' home.

Don Camillo was reading when Smilzo came in.

"There's a baptizing job for you to do," Smilzo said abruptly.

"A fine job indeed," muttered Don Camillo.

"Must one obtain a *nihil obstat* before having a baby?" Smilzo asked him.

"The *nihil obstat* of your own conscience," said Don Camillo. "But that's strictly your affair. Only if Moretta arrives dressed in her blue denims I'll chase you all away. You can come twenty minutes from now."

Moretta came with the baby in her arms and Smilzo at her side. Don Camillo received them along with Peppone and his wife at the door to the church.

"Take all that red stuff off," he said, without even looking to see if they really were wearing anything red. "This is the House of God and not the People's Palace."

"There's nothing red around here except the fog in your brain," muttered Peppone.

They went into the church and over to the baptismal font, where Don Camillo began the ceremony.

"What's the name?" he asked.

"Rita Palmira Valeria," the mother stated firmly.

There was a dead silence as the three names—every one of them of internationally famous Communists—echoed in the little church. Don Camillo replaced the cover on the font and was just about to say "then go and get her baptized in Russia" when he saw Christ looking down at him from the Cross. So he just took a deep breath and counted to ten instead.

"Rita is for my mother, Palmira for his and Valeria for my grandmother," Moretta pointed out.

"That's their bad luck," said Don Camillo dryly. "I say Emilia, Rosa, Antonietta."

Peppone pawed the ground, while Smilzo sighed and shook his head, but Moretta seemed secretly pleased.

Afterwards they went to the rectory to sign the register.

"Under the Christian Democrat government, is Palmira a forbidden name?" Peppone asked sarcastically.

Don Camillo did not answer, but motioned to him and his wife to go home. Smilzo, Moretta and the baby were left standing in front of the table.

"*Enciclica rerarum novium,*" said Smilzo more cleverly

:[129]:

than correctly, with the look of a man resigned to his fate.

"No, I'm not making a speech," Don Camillo said coldly. "I just want to give you a warning. By not getting married you are not hurting the Church. You're just two cockroaches trying to gnaw at one of the columns of Saint Peter's. Neither you nor your offspring are of the slightest interest to me."

At this moment the bundle in Moretta's arms stirred, and the "offspring" opened her eyes wide and smiled at Don Camillo. She had such a pink little face that Don Camillo paused and then his blood began to boil and he lost his temper.

"Miserable creatures!" he shouted. "You have no right to visit your foolish sins upon the head of this innocent baby. She's going to grow up to be a beautiful girl and when people are envious of her beauty they'll throw mud at her by calling her a 'kept woman's child.' If you weren't such wretches you wouldn't expose your daughter to people's jealous hypocrisy. You may not care what people say about you, but if on your account they slander her . . ."

Don Camillo had raised his fist and thrown out his chest so that he looked even taller and bigger than he was, and the two wretches had taken refuge in a corner.

"Get married, you criminals!" the priest shouted.

Pale and perspiring, Smilzo shook his head.

"No, that would be the end of everything for us. We couldn't face people."

The baby seemed to enjoy the scene. She waved her hands and laughed, and Don Camillo was taken aback.

"Please, I'm begging you!" he exclaimed. "She's too beautiful!"

Strange things can happen in this world. A man may try with a crowbar to force a door open and not move it a single inch. Then when he is dead tired and hangs his hat on the knob in order to wipe the sweat off his brow, click, the door opens. Moretta was a stubborn woman, but when she saw that Don

:[130]:

Camillo's anger was dying down as he looked at her baby, she threw herself onto a chair and began to cry.

"No, no," she sobbed. "We can't marry because we're married already. We did it three years ago, only nobody knows, because we did it some where far away. We've always liked free love. And so we've never told a soul."

Smilzo nodded.

"Marriage is the opium of love," he began. "Love was born free, and if God Almighty . . ."

Don Camillo went to douse his face in cold water. When he came back, Smilzo and his wife were quite calm, and Moretta was holding out a paper which was a marriage certificate.

"Under the secrecy of the confessional," she whispered.

Don Camillo nodded.

"So you've registered with your employer as 'single'," he said to Smilzo, "and you don't get any of the benefits of being a family man."

"Exactly," said Smilzo. "There's nothing I wouldn't do for my ideals."

Don Camillo handed back the certificate.

"You're two donkeys," he said calmly. Then, when the baby smiled, he corrected himself: "Two donkeys and a half."

Smilzo turned around at the door and raised a clenched fist in salute.

"There'll always be a place on the gallows for those who run down the people," he said gravely.

"You'd better hang your hat on it then, so as to reserve a place for yourself!" answered Don Camillo.

"The election we lost was just a passing phase," said Smilzo. "We have come from very far and we still have far to go. Farewell, citizen priest."

FOR SOME UNKNOWN reason Don Camillo had fallen into the habit of waking up in the middle of the night. He could hear nothing out of the ordinary, and yet he felt sure that there was something wrong. Finally, one night he heard a scuffling noise outside and, looking out the window, he saw a shadow moving about near the small side door of the church, below the tower. He must have made a noise, for the shadow slipped away. But the next night Don Camillo was better prepared. He left the window slightly open and laid his shotgun on the sill. Then at the last minute he gave up this plan.

"If it's someone trying to break into the church, then he isn't after me. That is, unless he's trying to place a time bomb inside."

This was a possibility, but one shouldn't impugn a stranger's intentions, even in the valley. And so Don Camillo finally decided to keep watch in the church. For three nights he played sentry in vain, and on the fourth night, when he was just about to give the whole thing up, he heard someone scraping at the lock of the side door. He kept perfectly still, and in a few minutes the lock sprang and the door slowly opened. There was no light in the church other than that given by a feeble sanctuary lamp, but Don Camillo made out the hesitant figure of a skinny young man. The man looked around him, found a ladder and cautiously raised it against the wall to the right of the altar. High along this wall were many offerings, in the form of silver hearts mounted in frames and hung as tokens of gratitude for some mark of divine favor. "So that's what you're after!" Don Camillo said to himself.

He let the intruder climb halfway up the ladder before he came out of an ambush, but Don Camillo was a big man and about as graceful in his movements as a division of armored cars so he made a tremendous racket. The man leaped down and tried to reach the door, but Don Camillo seized him by the nape of the neck. Then, in order to get a better hold, he let go the neck, caught the arms and raised them up in the air to make sure the fellow wasn't packing a gun. The fellow had crumpled up completely, and even if he had had a revolver on him he wouldn't have had the strength to pull the trigger. Don Camillo carried his catch into the sacristy, where he threw on the light and looked him in the face. When he saw who it was, he let him drop like a bundle of rags to the floor and sat down in front of him.

:[133]:

"Smilzo, you're no good as a thief, either!"

Smilzo shrugged his shoulders.

"It's not my trade," he answered, "I didn't mean to steal."

Don Camillo laughed.

"I don't suppose it was in order to say your prayers that you let yourself into the church with a pass-key in the middle of the night and started climbing up a ladder."

"Everyone prays in his own way," Smilzo protested.

"Well, you can explain it to the police," said Don Camillo.

This last word caused Smilzo to leap up, but Don Camillo simply stretched out one paw and put him down.

"Don't you get me into trouble," said Smilzo. "Here everything is tied up with politics, and that means a mess."

"Don't worry," Don Camillo reassured him. "This is a strictly criminal affair, and the charge will be attempted burglary."

Then he yanked the limp Smilzo to his feet and searched his pockets.

"Actual burglary!" he corrected himself. "This is the real thing!" And he held up what he had found.

"It isn't burglary at all," said Smilzo. "That belongs to me, and I paid for it with my own money."

The object was one of the votive offerings, a frame with a silver heart inside. Obviously it was brand new, but Don Camillo found it difficult to believe Smilzo's story and dragged him over to the wall where the ladder was still standing. Sure enough, nothing was missing. The offerings formed a perfect rectangle and the absence of even a single one would be noticed. Don Camillo examined the offering he had found in Smilzo's pocket. The heart was of sterling silver and carefully framed.

"Well then, what's it all about?" he asked. "How can you explain?"

Smilzo shrugged his shoulders.

:[134]:

"Gratitude is a good thing, but politics is filthy. I promised that if a certain deal came off, I'd offer one of these things to God. But since the Party and the Vatican are at swords' points, I couldn't afford to be seen. People might talk, because everyone knows you priests start them talking. Yes, when you warmongers . . ."

"Drop that," Don Camillo interrupted. "I know that whole spiel by heart. Let's stick to our present business. If you didn't want to be seen, you could have sent somebody. Why did you have to make such a detective story out of it?"

Smilzo puffed up his chest.

"We who come from the people always keep our word, even in matters of religion. I had promised to offer this thing in person and so I brought it. Now I shall hand it over to you."

In the valley close to the shore of the river they're all a little queer in the head, and after a few moments of reflection, Don Camillo gave up and threw out his arms.

"Very well," he said, "here's a receipt, and let's forget about it."

Smilzo slipped away from the foot Don Camillo had prepared for him and called back from the door.

"If you priests get through another year without being swept away by the rising tide of the people's revolution, you can thank God with one of these things ten feet square!"

Don Camillo was left with the silver heart in his hand, and took it to the altar to show to Christ.

"Lord, these people require understanding," he said. "They're less complex than one might think. They're simple, primitive souls, and even when they do something good they have to be violent about it. There are many things which we must forgive them."

"We must forgive them, indeed, Don Camillo," said Christ with a sigh.

Don Camillo was sleepy.

"I'll hang this up and not think about it any more until to-morrow," he said to himself. And he climbed up on the ladder and hung it just under the bottom row. Then he pulled out the nail he had just driven in and changed the location. "I'd better place it beside the one given by his wife. Whom God has joined together let no man put asunder, either in God's house or the Devil's."

Three months before, Smilzo's wife, Moretta, had been very ill and since the Party couldn't seem to heal her, she had turned to God. After an almost miraculous cure, she had brought an offering. Now Don Camillo leaned back and admired the two identical hearts.

"There's the same sinful soul in both bodies," he mumbled, shaking his head. After he had come down from the ladder he started to leave the church, but did not get as far as the door. He stopped short and went back to the altar.

"Lord, a man breaks into a church at two o'clock in the morning in order to hang up a votive offering. It simply doesn't make sense."

He paced up and down for a few minutes, then climbed up on the ladder again. He took down the two framed hearts and examined them under the light. Then he raised his head.

"We must indeed forgive them," Christ said with a smile.

Smilzo appeared at the rectory the next evening.

"I'm here on account of the same old story," he said with an indifferent air. "My wife's got it into her head that she must add two silver flowers to the offering she made three months ago. If you give it to me, I'll bring it back tomorrow."

"That's a good idea," said Don Camillo. "I have it right here. Last night, when I was hanging yours beside it, I saw that some dust had got under the glass and I took it down to clean it."

He opened a drawer of his desk and took out the offering given by Smilzo's wife. Then he reached for something else and showed it to Smilzo.

"Between the wooden frame and the velvet lining I found this object. I can't imagine how it got there. Is it yours?"

The object was Smilzo's Party membership card. Smilzo put out his hand, but Don Camillo slipped it back into the drawer.

"Well, what goes on?"

"It's not so funny," said Smilzo. "Moretta was about to die. She vowed she would give a silver heart and I promised a proletarian one. When she got well I put my Party card in with her offering, but at the last minute I didn't have the nerve to get out of the Party so I stayed in. Now Peppone wants to check all our cards. And it's no joking matter, the way it would be in Church or big business circles, where anything can be fixed with a little bribe. I'd be in serious trouble. So that's why I've got to get my card back."

Don Camillo slowly lit his cigar.

"Now the story makes sense," he said. "You had an exact duplicate of Moretta's offering made and sneaked into the church like a thief in order to switch them and rescue your Party card."

Smilzo shrugged his shoulders.

"I planned to return the offering the next day to take the place of the card, so you end up with two offerings instead of one," he said. "What use is a Party card to God, anyhow?"

Don Camillo raised his finger.

"A vow is a solemn obligation and you vowed . . ." he said.

"I'll fulfill it when the time comes," said Smilzo. "But I can't do it just now."

He seemed to be the same limp bundle of rags as the night before. Don Camillo took out the card and gave it to him.

:[137]:

"This filthy thing has no place in church," he said with scorn.

Smilzo put the card carefully into his wallet.

"Render unto Caesar that which is Caesar's, unto God that which is God's, and unto the people that which is the people's," he said as a parting shot.

"And unto Smilzo that which is Smilzo's!" added Don Camillo, giving him a hearty kick in the pants.

Smilzo took it with dignity.

"Come the revolution, those who have lifted a hand against the defenseless people will be paid back with interest," he proclaimed, "even when the hand happens to be a foot!"

Don Camillo went to hang up the hearts, and as he passed the altar he spread out his arms. Christ smiled.

"There are many things which we must forgive them, Don Camillo," he said. "On the Judgment Day none of them will carry a Party card on him."

Meanwhile Smilzo was walking proudly toward the People's Palace with his card in his pocket, feeling at peace with both God and man. Perhaps because what he had called his "proletarian heart" wasn't in his wallet, as he imagined, but in the votive offering to the right of the altar.

THE BICYCLE

IN THIS SLICE OF LAND
between the river and the highway it is hard to imagine a time
when the bicycle did not exist. Here in the valley, everyone
from five years old to eighty rides a bicycle. Little boys make
remarkable riders because they support themselves on bent
legs in the middle of the frame, and their bicycles move in
anything but a straight line, but they do move just the same.
The peasants for the most part use women's models, and the
paunchy landowners trundle along on old-fashioned contrap-

tions with a high seat which they reach by means of a little step screwed on to the rear axle.

City people's bicycles are utterly laughable. With gleaming metal gadgets, electric batteries, gearshifts, baskets, chain guards, speedometers and so on, they are mere toys and leg exercisers. A genuine bicycle should weigh at least sixty-five pounds; it should have lost most of its paint and at least one pedal. All that should be left of the remaining pedal is the shaft, rubbed smooth and shiny by the sole of the rider's shoe. Indeed, this should be its only shiny feature. The handlebars (with no rubber tips to them) should not be at the conventional right angle to the wheels, but inclined at least twelve degrees one way or the other. A genuine bicycle has no mudguard over the rear wheel, and hanging before the front mudguard there should be a piece of automobile tire, preferably red, to ward off splashes of water. A rear mudguard may be allowed when the rider is excessively disturbed by the streak of mud that accumulates on his back during a rainstorm. But in this case the mudguard must be split open in such a way that the rider can brake in so-called "American style," that is by pressing his trousercuffs against the rear wheel.

A Po valley bicycle has no mechanical brakes and its tires wear conspicuous patches, so protuberant as to impart to the wheels a spirited, jumping motion. In the little world a bicycle blends with the landscape; it would never try to be showy and beside it, those dressed up racing models are like third-rate chorus girls next to a substantial housewife. City people can't be expected to understand these things; where sentiments are concerned they are about as delicate as cows in clover. They live quite contentedly in their civic corruption, and never refer to their female poodles as bitches. They have what they call their "toilets" or "lavatories" right in the middle of the house, whereas every self-respecting countryman puts his honestly named "watercloset" in an outhouse at the far end of the courtyard. To locate this convenience next to one's eating or sleeping quarters is supposed to be a symbol of "Progress," but to leave it outdoors, where it is out of reach and lacking tiled walls and pavement, is to my mind cleaner and more truly civilized.

In the valley a bicycle is just as necessary as a pair of shoes, in fact more so. Because even if a man hasn't any shoes he can still ride a bicycle, whereas if he hasn't a bicycle he must surely travel on foot. This may hold true in the city as well, but in the city there are trolleys, while in the valley there are no rails of any kind, but only bicycle, motorcycle, and wagon tracks, cut every now and then by the trail of a snake that has slithered from one ditch to another.

Don Camillo had never been in business unless it is business to buy a pound of beef or a couple of black cigars and the accompanying box of what are locally called "lightning bolts," that is, sulphur matches to be struck on the soles of one's shoes or the seat of one's trousers. But if Don Camillo had never been in business, he enjoyed seeing it go on, and whenever Saturday was a fine day he mounted his bicycle and went to the weekly market at La Villa. He was interested in livestock, farm machinery, fertilizers, and sprays, and when he could buy a bag of copper sulphate with which to protect the grapevines behind the rectory he felt just about as happy as farmer Bidazzi with all his acres. There were all kinds of amusement stands in the marketplace and the holiday atmosphere and bustling activity never failed to put him in a good humor.

On this particular Saturday, then, Don Camillo got on his old bicycle and gaily ate up the seven miles to La Villa. The market was unusually crowded and Don Camillo got more fun out of it than if it had been the yearly fair at Milan. At

:⌈ 141 ⌉:

half-past eleven he went to get his bicycle from the lot where he had left it. He pulled it out by the handlebars and, working his way through all the confusion, started toward the narrow street leading to the open country. Here the Devil came into the picture, because Don Camillo stopped at a shop to buy some trifle, and when he came out, his bicycle, which he had left leaning against the wall, had disappeared.

Don Camillo was equipped with outsize bones and muscles. From his toes to the top of his head he was as tall as an ordinary man standing on a stool, and from the top of his head to his toes he was a hand's breadth taller, which means that although other people saw him as of one height he saw himself as of another, that is, his courage was a hand's breadth greater than his considerable physical stature! Even if someone were to have pulled a shotgun on him, his blood-pressure wouldn't have gone up a single degree. But if he stumbled over a stone in the road or someone played a trick upon him, he was unnerved by the humiliation. At such times he felt almost sorry for himself and positively melancholy.

Now, with his bicycle gone, he did not make a row. He asked an old man standing near by if he had seen anyone ride off on a woman's bicycle with a green basket. And when the man said no, he touched his hat and went away. He walked by the police station, but never thought of going in. The fact that a country priest, with twenty-five liras in his pocket, had been robbed of a bicycle was a private and moral problem, and not one to be introduced into the public domain. Your rich man, to whom it is all a matter of money, may rush to report a theft. But to the poor it is a personal injustice, in the same class as striking a cripple or knocking his crutch out from under him.

Don Camillo pulled his hat down over his eyes and started to walk home. Every time he heard a cart or wagon behind him, he ducked down at the side of the road. He wanted to go home under his own steam without having to talk to anybody. And he wanted to cover the whole seven miles on foot in order to underline the thief's guilt and his own sense of injury. He walked alone through the dust and heat for a solid hour without pause, brooding over the misfortunes of a Don Camillo who seemed to him to exist quite apart from himself. At a certain point a side road came into the one which he was traveling, and he stopped to lean on the wall of a small brick bridge. Leaning up against the same wall was his bicycle. He knew every inch of it, and there was no chance of any mistake. Immediately he looked around, but no one was in sight. He touched the bicycle and tapped the handlebars with his knuckles. Yes, they were of solid metal. The nearest house was at least half a mile away and the bushes were not yet covered with enough leaves to provide a hiding-place. Finally he looked over the wall of the bridge and saw a man sitting in the dried-up bed of the stream. The man stared up at him interrogatively.

"This bicycle is mine," Don Camillo said hesitatingly.

"What bicycle?"

"The one here against the wall of the bridge."

"Good," said the man. "If there's a bicycle on the bridge and it's your bicycle, that's not my business."

"I was just telling you," Don Camillo said, with considerable perplexity. "I didn't want there to be any mix-up about it."

"Are you sure it's yours?" the man asked.

"I should say I am! It was stolen from me while I was in a shop at La Villa an hour ago. I don't know how it got here."

The man laughed.

"It must have got bored waiting and gone ahead of you," he said.

Don Camillo threw out his arms in uncertainty.

"Are you, as a priest, able to keep a secret?" the man asked him.

"Certainly."

"Then I can tell you that the bicycle got here because I brought it here myself."

Don Camillo opened his eyes wide.

"Did you find it?"

"Yes, I found it in front of the shop. And I took it."

"Was that your idea of a joke?" asked Don Camillo, after another moment of hesitation.

"Don't be silly!" the man protested. "Do you think that at my age I go around joking? I meant to take it for keeps. Then I thought better of it and pedalled after you. I followed you up to about a mile back, then I took a shortcut, got here before you and put it right under your nose."

Don Camillo sat down on the wall and looked at the fellow below him.

"Why did you take the bicycle if it wasn't yours?" he asked.

"Everyone to his own trade. You deal in souls and I deal in bicycles."

"Has that been your trade for long?"

"No, just for the last two or three months. I operate at markets and fairs, and I usually do pretty well, because a lot of these peasants have stone jars full of banknotes. This morning I had no luck, and so I took your bicycle. Then I saw you come out of the shop and go your way without telling anybody. I began to be sorry and followed you, I still don't understand exactly why. Why did you duck down every time a wagon caught up with you? Did you know I was behind you?"

"No."

"Well, I was. And if you'd accepted a lift, I'd have turned back. But since you kept on walking I had to follow."

Don Camillo shook his head. "Where are you going now?" he asked.

"Back to see if there's anything doing at La Villa."

"To see if you can lay hands on another bicycle."

"Of course."

"Then keep this one."

The man looked up at him.

"Not on your life, Father. Not even if it were made of solid gold. It would be on my conscience and ruin my career. I prefer to stay clear of the clergy."

Don Camillo asked if he had had anything to eat, and the man said no.

"Then come eat something with me."

A wagon came by, and in it rode a peasant called Brelli.

"Come along, you wretch!" said Don Camillo. "You take the bicycle and I'll go in the wagon."

Then he stopped Brelli and told him that he had a pain in his leg. The man came up from below the bridge. He was so angry that he threw his cap on the ground and cursed a large number of saints before he got on the bicycle.

Don Camillo had had the meal ready for ten minutes by the time the bicycle thief arrived at the rectory.

"There's only bread, sausage, cheese, and a drop of wine," said the priest. "I hope that's enough for you."

"Don't worry, Father," said the man. "I've taken care of that." And put a chicken on the table.

"The creature was crossing the road and I accidentally ran over it," he explained. "I didn't want to leave it to die there, and so I put an end to its pain . . . Don't look at me like that, Father. I'm sure that if you broil it properly, God will forgive you."

Don Camillo broiled the chicken and brought out a bottle of special wine. After an hour or so, the man said he must be about his business, but there was a worried look on his face.

"I don't know how I can go back to stealing bicycles," he sighed. "You've demoralized me completely."

"Have you a family?" Don Camillo asked him.

"No, I'm all alone."

"Then I'll take you on as a bell-ringer. Mine just went away two days ago."

"But I don't know how to ring bells."

"A man who knows how to steal bicycles won't find that hard to learn."

And he was bell-ringer from that day on.

ONE DAY DON CAMILLO
was in the church talking things over with Christ and at a certain point he said:

"Lord, too many things in this world are out of kilter."

"I don't see it that way," Christ answered. "Man may be out of kilter, but the rest of the universe works pretty well."

Don Camillo paced up and down and then stopped again in front of the altar.

"Lord," he said, "if I were to start counting: one, two, three, four, five, six, seven, and count for a million years,

:[147]:

should I ever come to a point where there were no more numbers?"

"Never," said Christ. "You remind me of the man who drew a big circle on the ground and began to walk around it, saying: 'I want to see how long it will take me to get to the end.' So I must tell you: 'No, you'd never come to such a point.' "

In his imagination, Dom Camillo was walking around the circle and feeling the breathlessness that must stem from a first glance into infinity.

"I still say that numbers must be finite," he insisted. "Only God is infinite and eternal, and numbers can't claim to have the attributes of God."

"Why have you got it in for numbers?" Christ asked him.

"Because numbers are what have put men out of kilter. Having discovered numbers, they've proceeded to deify them."

When Don Camillo got an idea into his head, there was no getting it out. He locked the main door of the church for the night, paced up and down some more, and then came back to the altar.

"Perhaps, Lord, men's reliance upon the magic of numbers is just a desperate attempt to justify their existence as thinking beings." He remained uneasily silent for a minute and then went on: "Lord, are ideas finite? Are there no new ideas or have men thought up everything there is to be thought?"

"Don Camillo, what do you mean by ideas?"

"As a poor country priest, all I can say is that ideas are lamps shining through the night of human ignorance and lighting up some new aspect of the greatness of the Creator."

Christ smiled.

"Poor country priest," He said, "you're not so far from right. Once a hundred men were shut into an enormous dark room, each one of them with an unlit lamp. One of them managed to light his lamp, and so they all could see one another and get to know one another. As the rest lit their lamps, more

:[148]:

and more of the objects around them came into view, until finally everything in the room stood out as good and beautiful. Now, follow me closely, Don Camillo, there were a hundred lamps, only one idea; yet it took the light of all the lamps to reveal the details of everything in the room. Every flame was the hundredth part of one great idea, one great light, the idea of the existence and majesty of the Creator. It was as if a man had broken a statuette into a hundred pieces and given one piece to each of a hundred men. The hundred men groped for one another and tried to fit the fragments together, making thousands of misshapen figures until at last they joined them properly. I repeat, Don Camillo, that every man lit his own lamp and the light of the hundred lamps together was Truth and Revelation. This should have satisfied them. But each man thought that the beauty of the objects he saw around him was due to the light of his own lamp, which had brought them out of the darkness. Some men stopped to worship their own lamps, and others wandered off in various directions, until the great light was broken up into a hundred flames, each one of which could illuminate only a fraction of the truth. And so you see, Don Camillo, that the hundred lamps must come together again in order to find the true light. Today men wander mistrustfully about, each one in the light of his own lamp, with an area of melancholy darkness all around him, clinging to the slightest detail of whatever object he can illuminate by himself. And so I say that ideas do not exist; there is only one Idea, one Truth with a hundred facets. Ideas are neither finite nor finished, because there is only this one and eternal Idea. But men must join their fellows again like those in the enormous room."

Don Camillo threw out his arms.

"There's no going back," he sighed. "Today men use the oil of their lamps to grease their filthy machines and machine guns."

Christ smiled.

"In the Kingdom of Heaven," He said, "oil is so bountiful it runs in rivers."

In the rectory Don Camillo found Brusco waiting. Brusco was Peppone's right-hand man, a big fellow who opened his mouth only when he had something important to say. He spat out an average of no more than ten or fifteen words a day.

"Somebody must be dead. Who is it?" Don Camillo asked him.

"Nobody. But I'm in trouble."

"Did you kill somebody by mistake?"

"No, it's on account of my son."

"Which one? Falchetto?"

"No, none of the eight that are here at home. The one that's been in Sicily all these years."

Don Camillo remembered that in 1938 one of Brusco's sisters, who had married a man with land holdings in Sicily, had come to visit him. Before going home she had lined up Brusco's nine children.

"Can I have one?" she asked him.

"Take whichever one you like best."

"I'll take the least dirty of the lot."

And her choice fell upon Cecotto, who happened to have just washed his face. He was about eight years old and somehow different from the rest.

"Let's be quite frank if we want to stay friends," said Brusco's sister. "I'll take him and bring him up and you'll never see him again."

Brusco's wife had just died, and to be relieved of responsibility for one of his nine children was a blessing from Heaven. He nodded assent and only when his sister was at the door did he tug at her sleeve and say:

:[150]:

"Do you mind taking Falchetto instead?"

"I wouldn't have him even as a gift," she answered, as if she had paid hard cash for Cecotto.

Don Camillo remembered the whole story.

"Well then?" he asked.

"I haven't seen him for twelve years," said Brusco, "but he's always written to me, and now he says he's coming home for a visit."

Don Camillo looked at him hard.

"Brusco, has the Five-year Plan gone to your head? Is it such a misfortune to see your son? Are you Reds ashamed of your own children?"

"No, I'm not ashamed even of Falchetto, who's one of the biggest cowards I've ever known. It's my fault, not his, if he's turned out the way he has. This is an entirely different matter. In Sicily they're all reactionaries of one kind or another: barons, landowners, priests and so on. Of course, a son's a son, no matter what he does. But if he comes here I'll fall into disgrace with the Party. I should have let the Party know about the whole situation . . ."

Don Camillo could hold himself back no longer.

"Come on and let the cat out of the bag!" he exclaimed. "What has the poor fellow done?"

Brusco lowered his head.

"They sent him to school . . ." he muttered.

"Well, you're not ashamed of him for that, are you?"

"No, but he's studying for the priesthood."

Don Camillo couldn't help laughing.

"So your son's a priest! That's a good one! A priest!"

"Pretty nearly one. . . . But take it easy, will you?"

Don Camillo had never heard Brusco speak in just this tone of voice. He waited to hear more.

"If he comes here, and Peppone catches on, he'll kill me.

:[151]:

And since the boy's a priest, or nearly, I don't want him to know that I'm on the other side. You priests understand one another. And if you can't fix things up, I'm done for. He's arriving at eight o'clock tomorrow."

"All right. Let me sleep on it."

Brusco had never thanked anyone in his life.

"I'll make it up to you," he muttered. And he added, from the door: "I have the worst luck! With all the reactionaries there are around, why did I have to have a priest for a son?"

Don Camillo was not in the least discomfited.

"With all the rogues there are available, why did a poor priest have to be cursed with a Communist father?"

Brusco shook his head.

"Everyone has his own troubles," he said with a bitter sigh.

SHOTGUN WEDDING

WHENEVER DON CAMILLO
saw old man Rocchi come to the church or the rectory he
grumbled to himself: "Here's the commissar." For old man
Rocchi was the leader of the watchdogs who appoint themselves in every parish to scrutinize the conduct of the priest,
in church and out of it, and to write letters of protest to the
bishop when they find it shocking or even improper. Of course
the old man never missed a single service, and since he and his
family occupied one of the front pews he followed everything
Don Camillo said and did, and would turn to say to his wife

in the middle of Mass: "He skipped something," or: "Today he's not got his wits about him," or: "Don Camillo isn't what he used to be." And he would go to the rectory afterwards to comment upon the sermon and give Don Camillo some sound advice.

Don Camillo wasn't the type to worry about such things, but it was a bother to feel old Rocchi's eyes constantly upon him and whenever he had to blow his nose in the middle of Mass he raised his eyes to Christ on the cross above the altar and silently prayed: "Lord help me blow my nose in a manner that will not cause a scandal!" For Rocchi was a great stickler for form. More than once he had remarked: "When the priest at Treville has to blow his nose in the middle of Mass, nobody knows it, but this one sounds like a trumpet calling to the Last Judgment."

That is the kind of a man Rocchi was, and if such men exist in the world it must mean that they have a place to fill in it. He had three sons and one daughter, Paolina, who was the most virtuous and most beautiful girl in the village. And it was Paolina that startled Don Camillo almost out of his wits one day in the confessional.

"I can't grant you absolution before you do what you are supposed to," he told her.

"I know," said the girl.

This is the sort of thing that happens in every village, and in order to understand it one really has to have lived in one of the low houses in the broad valley and to have seen the moon rise like a great red ball over the bank of the river. There is no visible movement in the valley and a stranger may have the idea that nothing ever happens along the deserted river banks, that nothing *could* happen in the red and blue houses. Yet more things happen there than up in the mountains or in the big city. For the blazing summer sun gets into people's

veins, and that big red moon is utterly unlike the pale satellite
hey see in other places; it blazes just like the sun, inflaming
the imaginations of the living and the bones of the dead. Even
in winter, when the valley is filled with cold and fog, the heat
stored up during the summer is so great that people's imaginations aren't cooled off sufficiently to see things as they ac-
ually are. That is why every now and then a shotgun peeps out
of a thicket or a girl does something she oughtn't do.

Paolina went home, and when the family had finished saying the evening rosary she stepped up to her father.

"Father, I must have a talk with you," she said.

The others went their various ways and Paolina and her
father were left beside the fire.

"What's it all about?" asked the old man suspiciously.

"It's time to think about my getting married."

"Don't you bother your head about that. When the time
comes, we'll find the right sort of fellow."

"The time has already come, Father, and I've found him."

The old man opened his eyes wide.

"Go straight to bed, and don't let me hear you talk of such
things again!" he ordered.

"Very well," said the girl, "but you'll hear other people
talking about them."

"Have you given some cause for scandal?" asked the hor-
ified father.

"No, but the scandal will come out. It's not something that
can be concealed."

Rocchi took hold of the first thing that came to hand, which
happened to be a broken broomstick. The girl crouched in a
corner, hiding her head, and received a rain of blows upon
her back. Luckily the broomstick broke again and her father
quieted down.

"If you're so unlucky as to be still alive, get up," he told
her. "Does anyone know about it?"

"*He* knows . . ." murmured the girl, causing the old man to lose his head again and start to beat her with a stick taken from a bundle of faggots by the fire. "And so does Don Camillo," she added. "He wouldn't grant me absolution." Again the old man took it out on her. Finally she got in another word: "If you kill me, it will be an even worse scandal," she said, and that calmed him.

"Who's the man?" he asked.

"Falchetto," she answered.

She would have produced less of an effect if she had named Beelzebub in person. Falchetto was the nickname of Gigi Bariga, one of the most stalwart of Peppone's henchmen. He was the intellectual member of the gang, the one who wrote speeches, organized rallies and explained the Party directives. Because he understood more than the others, he was the unholiest of them all. The girl had taken so much punishment by now that the old man pushed her onto a couch and sat down beside her.

"You've beaten me enough," she said. "If you touch me again, I'll call for help and tell everybody. I have to protect the life of my child."

At eleven o'clock that night the old man gave in to his fatigue.

"I can't kill you, and in the state you're in, you can't very well enter a convent," he said. "Marry, then, and be damned both of you."

When Falchetto saw the effects of Paolina's beating his jaw dropped.

"We must get married," she said, "or this will be the death of me."

"Of course!" said Falchetto. "That's what I've been asking you all along. Right away, if you give the word, Paolina."

:[156]:

It was no use thinking of marriage at quarter to one in the morning, but words exchanged at the garden gate, before the fields covered with snow, had a certain value and significance.

"Have you told your father everything?" Falchetto asked.

She did not answer, and Falchetto realized that it was a stupid question.

"I'll take my Tommy gun and shoot up your entire family," he exclaimed. "I'll . . ."

"There's no need to shoot. All we have to do is go get the priest's permission."

Falchetto stepped back.

"You know I can't do that," he said. "Just think of my position. We can go to the mayor."

The girl pulled her shawl around her.

"No, never," she said. "I don't care about what may happen. Either we are married like Christians or else I'll never see you again."

"Paolina! . . ." Falchetto implored her, but she had already slipped through the gate in the opposite direction from that which she had so often taken before.

Paolina stayed in bed for two days, and on the third day her father came up to her room.

"You saw him the other evening," he said: "I happen to know."

"So do I."

"Well, then?"

"Nothing doing. He won't have a Christian wedding. And I say a Christian wedding or nothing at all."

The other man shouted and stamped his feet. Then he left his daughter, threw his overcoat over his shoulders and went out. And a few minutes later Don Camillo had a difficult problem before him.

"Father, you already know the story," said Rocchi.

"I do. Children need looking after. It's a parent's job to give them some moral principles."

Rocchi was properly put in his place, and he would gladly have strangled Don Camillo.

"I've consented to the marriage, but the rascal won't have anything to do with the Church."

"That doesn't surprise me."

"I've come to ask you this: is it more scandalous for a girl in my daughter's condition to marry outside the Church or not to marry at all?"

Don Camillo shook his head.

"This isn't a question of scandal. It's a question of good or evil. We must consider the unborn child."

"All I care about is to get them married and let them be damned!" said Rocchi.

"Then why do you ask for my advice? If all you care about is to get them married, let them marry as they please."

"But she says if she can't have a church wedding she'll have none at all," groaned the unhappy father.

Don Camillo smiled.

"You ought to be proud of your daughter. Two wrongs don't make a right. I say she has a head on her shoulders and you ought to be proud of her."

"I'll have to kill her, that's all," Rocchi shouted as he left the rectory.

"You don't expect me to argue the girl out of a church wedding, do you?" Don Camillo shouted back after him.

During the night Paolina heard a hail of pebbles against her window and finally her resistance was overcome and she went down. Falchetto was waiting, and when she saw his face she burst into tears.

"I've left the Party," he told her. "Tomorrow they'll get

out an announcement of my expulsion. Peppone wanted me to write it myself."

The girl went closer to him.

"Did he beat you up?" she asked.

"I thought he'd never stop," Falchetto admitted. "When are we going to get married?"

"Right away, if you give the word," she said. And her impulse was just as foolish as his, because it was almost one o'clock in the morning and poor Falchetto had one eye as black as a lump of coal.

"I'll talk to the priest about it tomorrow," he said. "But I won't go near the town hall. I don't want to see Peppone."

He touched his black eye and Paolina put a hand on his shoulder.

"We'll go to the mayor, too," she said. "I'll be there to stick up for you."

Paolina went early the next morning to Don Camillo.

"You can grant me absolution," she told him. "I didn't do any of the things I confessed to you. My only sin is to have told you a big lie."

Don Camillo was puzzled, but she quickly explained.

"If I hadn't made up that story, my father would never have let me marry Falchetto."

Don Camillo shook his head.

"Don't tell him the truth at this point," he advised her, secretly thinking that old man Rocchi had it coming to him.

"No, I won't tell him, not even after we're married," said the girl. "He beat me just as hard as if what I told him had been true."

"That's what I say," chimed in Don Camillo. "Such a beating shouldn't be given in vain."

As he passed by the altar, Christ frowned down at him.

"Lord," said Don Camillo, "Whosoever shall exalt himself

shall be humbled and he that shall humble himself shall be exalted."

"Don Camillo," said Christ, "for some time now you've been skating on thin ice."

"With God's help no ice is too thin," said Don Camillo. "This wedding will be worth a dozen of the usual kind."

And so it was.

SEEDS OF HATE

Peppone Popped up in front of Don Camillo without any warning, followed by Smilzo, Bigio, Brusco, and Lungo. It looked like revenge or intimidation, and Don Camillo's first thought was of Falchetto, who had left the Party to marry Rocchi's daughter. "They're furious because they imagine I had something to do with it," he said to himself. But the gang wasn't thinking of Falchetto at all.

"There's no God in this, and no politics either," said Peppone, puffing like a trolley car on the Mulino Nuovo hill.

"This is a patriotic matter. I'm here in my capacity of citizen mayor and you in your capacity of citizen priest."

Don Camillo spread out his arms in welcome.

"Speak, citizen mayor! The citizen priest is all ears."

Peppone stood in front of the table where Don Camillo was sitting, while his followers silently lined up behind him with their legs wide apart and their arms crossed over their chests.

"The Nemesis of History . . ." Peppone began, somewhat to Don Camillo's alarm, ". . . and not only the Nemesis of History but the Nemesis of Geography as well, and if that isn't enough . . ."

"I think it *is* enough," said Don Camillo, feeling reassured by the addition of Geography. "Just tell me what it's all about."

Peppone turned toward his followers with an indignant and ironical smile.

"They claim independence and home rule," he said, "and yet they don't know what's going on a mere fifty yards away."

"They're still living in the egotistical Middle Ages," said Smilzo unctuously. *"Cicero pro domo sua* and let the people eat cake!"

Don Camillo looked up at him.

"Are they teaching you Latin now?" he asked.

"Why not?" Smilzo retorted. "Do you think you have a monopoly on culture?"

But Peppone interrupted this exchange.

"They're a bunch of unpatriotic scoundrels, who want to usurp the sacred rights of the people by setting up an utterly unfounded claim to independence. I'm speaking of those wretched citizens of Fontanile, who want to secede from our township and set up a village administration of their own. We must nip their attempt in the bud by a manifesto outlining from A to Z the historical and geographical Nemesis which

:[162]:

makes this town their capital city and their miserable village a mere suburb or dependency . . ."

The discovery of what Peppone meant by "historical and geographical Nemesis" was not completely reassuring after all. Don Camillo knew his river valley and was aware of the fact that when two of its communities started to bicker, even on the basis of such a big word as "nemesis," it was no laughing matter. Between these two in particular there was considerable unfinished business. And for some time the inhabitants of Fontanile had had this home-rule bug in their bonnets. They had struck the first blow in 1902, when three or four groups of four houses each had put together the money to erect a public building, complete with arcade, sweeping stairway, clock tower and coat-of-arms over the door. This was to be the town hall. Then there was such an internal row about it that the police were called in and several citizens went to jail. That was as far as they got then. But the building remained and it was never put to any other use. They tried again in 1920, just after the First World War, but with no more success. And this was a third attempt. Don Camillo proceeded to feel his way cautiously.

"Have you tried talking to them about it?" he asked.

"Me talk to them?" shouted Peppone. "The only language I can make them understand is the Tommy gun."

"It doesn't seem as if negotiations would get very far on that basis," observed Don Camillo.

Peppone couldn't have been any angrier if his status had been lowered to that of a feudal serf.

"We'll act in strictly democratic fashion," he said with painful deliberation. "We'll draw up a statement explaining the historical and geographical Nemesis, and if they're too dense to understand it . . ."

Here Peppone paused, and Bigio, who was the best balanced of the gang, put in somberly: "If they don't understand, we'll start pushing them around."

When the slow-going Bigio spoke in these terms, it meant that things were close to the boiling point. Don Camillo tried another tack.

"If they want to secede, why not let them do it? What do you care?"

"It doesn't matter to me personally," shouted Peppone, "but it's an attack on the sovereignity of the people. This is the seat of the township. If we lose Fontanile and some of the territory beyond La Rocchetta, what's left? What sort of a whistle stop would this be? Are you by any chance unpatriotic too?"

Don Camillo sighed.

"Why turn it into a tragedy? Fontanile has never been allowed to set itself up as an independent village, has it? Why should the authorities allow it to do so now? There's no change in the situation."

Peppone brought his fist down on the table.

"That's what *you* say!" he shouted ironically. "There's a political factor involved. Our Party is entrenched in the town hall and over at Fontanile they're all reactionaries. So the national government would be glad to see some of our land and our people fall under a different administration!"

Don Camillo looked at him hard.

"You're the citizen mayor and in politics up to your ears so you ought to know. As a mere citizen priest, I'm in the dark."

Smilzo came forward and pointed an accusing finger at him. "You hireling of the Americans!" he said cuttingly.

Don Camillo shrugged his shoulders.

"Well what are we going to do?" he asked Peppone.

"The first thing is to draw up a manifesto embodying our historicial, geographical and economic arguments."

:[164]:

"And where am I to find them?" asked Don Camillo.

"That's up to you. Didn't they teach you anything at the seminary except how to make propaganda for America? . . . After that we'll see. If they drop their plan, all right; if they don't, we'll send them an *intimatum* to the effect that either they drop it or else . . . or else the will of the people shall decide!"

"God's will, you mean," Don Camillo corrected him.

"God doesn't come into this, we've said that already," replied Peppone. "But I'll take care of the *intimatum*, anyhow."

Don Camillo spent half the night putting together a manifesto of the reasons why Fontanile should not set itself up as an independent village. The hardest part was to reconcile the conflicting points of view and not to tread on anybody's toes. Finally the manifesto was sent to the printer and then a group of young men went to paste it up at Fontanile.

At noon the next day a box was delivered to Peppone at the town hall. It contained one of the posters that had been pasted up at Fontanile the night before, and rolled up inside was something extremely unpleasant. Peppone wrapped it up again and hurried over to the rectory, where he unfolded it in front of Don Camillo.

"Here is the answer from Fontanile," he said.

"Very well," said Don Camillo. "I wrote the statement, so that's meant for me. Leave it here and don't think about it anymore."

Peppone shook his head. He folded it up again and started to go silently away. But at the door he turned around.

"Citizen priest," he said, "you'll soon have plenty of work to do."

Don Camillo was so taken aback that he could find nothing to answer. Peppone's words had transfixed him with fear.

"Lord," he said to Christ at the altar. "Haven't war and politics put enough hate into these men's hearts?"

"Unfortunately they can always find room for more," Christ sighed.

M

ESSENGERS WERE COM-
ing and going at the town hall all day long, and Don Camillo
could not make out what those devils were up to, especially as
everybody claimed not to know. But toward nine o'clock in the
evening, when he was preparing to go to bed, someone knocked
at the shutter of the window on the Church square. It was
Smilzo, who said at once: "You've got to come to the town hall
immediately. Hurry up, because the people have no time to
wait upon the convenience of the clergy."

Smilzo was even more peremptory than usual. He felt that

he could be so quite safely with the grating of the window between Don Camillo and himself, and furthermore his tone of voice made it plain that he believed that he was entrusted with an unusually important mission.

"What do you mean by the people?" Don Camillo asked him. "People like yourself?"

"I didn't come here for a political discussion. If you're afraid to come out of your lair, that's another matter."

Don Camillo threw on his coat and picked up an umbrella, because just for a change it was raining.

"May I be told what's going on?" he asked along the way.

"It's not something that can be discussed on the street," said Smilzo. "That's just as if I were to ask you about the latest secret instructions sent you by the Pope."

"Leave the Pope alone," said Don Camillo, "or I'll break this umbrella over your head. The Pope has nothing to do with it."

"Whether he does or doesn't is something that we shall see about later, come the revolution," said Smilzo. "But never mind about that just now. You'll see what's going on when we reach the Town Hall."

Before they arrived a sentry halted them.

"Give the password," said a voice.

"*Venezia,*" said Smilzo.

"*Milano,*" came the reply.

Once they were by, Don Camillo asked what was the meaning of all this nonsense, but Smilzo said that it wasn't nonsense at all.

"It's war," he maintained.

When they walked into the council room, Don Camillo was very much surprised. The place was full of people, and not people to be dismissed as unimportant, either. All the notables of the village were there, representing all shades of political opinion, with nobody missing. There was a sepulchral silence, and evidently they were waiting for Don Camillo, for when he came in, they made way before him. Then Peppone stood up and gave an explanation.

"Father," he said, "at this tragic time, when our country is in danger, you see here before you our most representative citizens, without distinction of party; farmers, workers, land-owners, and shopkeepers, all joined in one faith. The attempt of an irresponsible group to trespass on our sacred rights must be defeated at any cost whatsoever . . . and so far I believe we all agree."

"Good," was the crowd's unanimous reply.

"In order to do away with any suspicion of party intrigue, the representatives of every faction have decided to choose someone who shall impartially pass upon every decision made by the Committee for Public Safety for the defense of the village. By a secret ballot you were elected, and so, overcoming our political differences, we call upon you to be a member of the Committee in the role of neutral observer."

"I accept," said Don Camillo, looking around him, and the crowd applauded him loudly.

"We welcome your help. Here, then, is the situation. The people of Fontanile have answered our statement, duly approved by the representative of the Vatican here present, in an insulting and anti-democratic manner. In short, they have defied their capital city."

An angry murmur arose from the audience.

"Yes!" shouted Peppone. "On historical, geographical, and economic grounds we may call our village the spiritual capital of the whole township, a capital one and indivisible forever."

"Well spoken!" called the crowd.

Peppone had now swung into high gear and was going full speed ahead.

"Strengthened by this gathering's lofty spirit of concord

:[169]:

and comprehension, we say that we will not tolerate the 'home-rulers' of Fontanile, in their attempt to secede from our township and set up a village administration of their own. We suggest sending them an *intimatum* to say: Either drop the idea or we'll make you drop it. Because democracy is all very well, but when you're dealing with a bunch of people like those at Fontanile . . ."

Peppone was so swollen with rage that he looked even bigger and stronger than usual and his audience stared at him in fascination. Unfortunately, with the word "Fontanile" his vocabulary suddenly gave out and he could not find another word to say. He was standing on a two-inch-thick telephone book, and he seized upon this and slowly twisted it in his hands until it was torn in two. In the river valley an argument of this kind is invariably decisive. The assembly let out a yell of enthusiasm, and when Peppone threw the two parts of the book on the table before him, crying: "And this is our *intimatum!*" the applause threatened to bring down the ceiling. When quiet once more prevailed, Peppone turned to Don Camillo.

"Will the neutral observer give us the benefit of his opinion?"

Don Camillo got up and said calmly but in a loud voice: "My opinion is that you're all crazy."

His words were like an icy wind, and a heavy silence fell over the gathering.

"You've lost all sense of reality and proportion," Don Camillo continued. "It's as if you were building a skyscraper on a six-inch foundation, with the result that the whole thing will topple down on you. It isn't a question of sending ultimatums or tearing telephone books in two. We must use our heads, and if we do so it is clear that there's no use even discussing the matter until the authorities give Fontanile permission to secede."

"But we're the authorities," shouted Peppone. "This is a matter for our concern."

Looking at the assembly, Don Camillo saw old man Rocchi rise from his seat in the front row.

"We agree, Father," said Rocchi, "that we should act calmly and not dramatize the situation. But if we wait for the authorities to give their permission, then our protest will be a revolt against the government. We must, in orderly fashion, of course, prevent Fontanile from putting in any request for home rule. I think the mayor is wrong to speak of using force, but the substance of what he says is right."

"Good!" came voices from the assembly. "The mayor has the right idea, even if we belong to different political parties. Politics doesn't come into this at all; it's the welfare of the village that's at stake. And let's be frank. We know what sort of people they are in Fontanile, and this is something we can't stand for."

Peppone shot a triumphant glance at Don Camillo and Don Camillo threw out his arms in dismay.

"It's a sad fact," he said, "but people seem to agree only when it comes to doing something very foolish. But before carrying things too far, the two parties to the dispute must have a discussion. We must send a committee over to Fontanile."

"Of course," said Rocchi, and all the others nodded assent.

Peppone had no more telephone books to which he could give a "twister," but he took something out of the drawer of the table. This was the famous and insulting answer from Fontanile.

"How can you 'discuss' anything with people like these?" he asked.

At that the crowd became very restless.

"Even an *intimatum* would be too good for the likes of

them," said farmer Sacchini, shaking his big stick. "This is the only language they can understand."

Don Camillo felt himself entirely alone.

"It's no use my asking God to illuminate your minds," he cried, "because it's plain you haven't any. But I say that you simply can't do any of these things you propose."

"Who'll stop us?" asked Peppone.

"I will," said Don Camillo. He went resolutely to the door and then turned around while he put up his umbrella. "I'm going straight to the police sergeant," he said. "That may change your plans."

"You spy!" Peppone shouted, pointing an accusing finger at him from the platform. The crowd formed a wall between Don Camillo and Peppone, and the priest had no alternative but to go straight to the police station.

The forces of the law, consisting of the sergeant and four men, were put on watch, half at Fontanile and half in the "capital city." The sergeant, since he could not be split in two, rode on his bicycle to reënforce first one squad and then the other. Three days went by and nothing happened.

"It's clear that they've thought better of it," the sergeant said to Don Camillo. "They seem to have calmed down."

"Here's hoping God gave them minds and then illuminated them," Don Camillo replied without much conviction.

But on the afternoon of the fourth day an ugly incident took place at a big farm known as Case Nuove. A group of unemployed farm laborers swarmed over the place in bicycles, saying that they must be given work. Among other things, their claim was a stupid one, for it had rained for ten days in succession and the only work anyone could do in the fields was to walk a couple of yards and then sink up to the hips in mud. Obviously it was a trouble-making political maneuver. But for fear the farmer or some of his family

:[172]:

might pull out a shotgun, the sergeant had to despatch his men to the spot. Toward evening Don Camillo went to look the situation over. The farm had been cleared of intruders, and these were wandering about in small groups not far away.

"If we leave, they'll be back in five minutes and start more trouble," said the sergeant. "Night is coming, and that's a tricky time where something like this is concerned."

Don Camillo ran into one of the groups on his way home and recognized among it the tailor from Molinetto.

"Have you changed your trade?" the priest asked him, "and turned into an unemployed farm laborer?"

"If people weren't so inquisitive, it would be a very fine thing," grumbled the tailor.

A little farther on Don Camillo met the old postman riding a bicycle, with a tool-box slung around his shoulder, which served him for his supplementary job as linesman for the telephone and telegraph systems. The priest was surprised to see him out so late, but the old man explained:

"I'm having a look around. The storm must have brought down a wire somewhere. Neither the telephone nor the telegraph is working."

Instead of going back to the rectory, Don Camillo went to Brelli's house. He wrote a hurried note and gave it to the youngest boy to deliver.

"Take your motorcycle and get this to the parish priest at Villetta as fast as you can. It's a matter of life and death."

The boy was off like a flash. An hour later he came back to report: "The priest said he'd telephone right away."

The river was swollen with rain and pressing against its banks. So were all the tributaries that poured into it across the plain. In normal weather these streams are ridiculous affairs. Either their beds are completely dry or else they con-

:[173]:

tain only a few spoonfuls of water and one wonders why people with any sense should throw away money building up banks on either side. But they are not only ridiculous; they are unpredictable as well, like an ordinarily temperate man who once in a while goes out and gets . . . well, dead drunk is too mild a phrase for it. When these valley streams rise, they are so many Mississippis, with the water surging halfway up their banks and over. Now, after the prolonged storm, even the tiniest streams were frighteningly high and people went along the banks measuring their height with a stick. And the water continued to rise.

Fontanile was divided from the "capital" by just such a stream, and for twenty years no one had seen so much water in it. Night had fallen, but Don Camillo paced nervously up and down the road leading along the bank. His nervousness did not pass until he heard the brakes of a big car. The car was full of policemen, and with their arrival Don Camillo went back to the rectory and hung his shotgun on the wall. After supper Peppone came to see him, looking very glum.

"Did you call the police?" he asked Don Camillo.

"Of course I did, after you staged that diversion at Case Nuove in order to have a free hand for your other mischief, yes, and after you cut the telephone and telegraph wires, too."

Peppone looked at him scornfully.

"You're a traitor!" he said. "You asked for foreign aid. A man without a country, that's what you are!"

This was such a wild accusation that Don Camillo was left gaping. But Peppone had still more to say.

"You're positively Godless!" he exclaimed, "but your police won't get anywhere. In two minutes God's justice will triumph!"

Don Camillo leaped to his feet, but before he could say a word there was a loud roar in the distance.

"The bank at Fontanile has given way," Peppone explained. "A concealed wire attached to a mine did the job. Now that Fontanile is flooded, they can found a little Venice if they want to!"

Don Camillo grabbed Peppone by the neck, but before he could squeeze it there came another roar, followed by a splash of water. A moment later the rectory was flooded. When the water had reached the two men's belts it stopped rising.

"Do you see what murderers they are?" Peppone shouted. "So this was their little plan!"

Don Camillo looked sadly at the liquid mess, then shook his head and sighed.

"Dear God, if this is the beginning of the Great Flood, then I bless you for wiping this idiotic human race off the face of the globe."

But Peppone didn't see it the same way.

"*Navigare necessariorum est!*" he shouted, wading toward the door. "Italy's manifest destiny is on the seven seas!"

"Then all we have to do is wait for low tide," concluded Don Camillo philosophically.

There were three feet of water in the church, and when the candles were lit on the altar they cast the reflection of their flames into the water.

"Lord," said Don Camillo to the crucified Christ, "I beg your forgiveness, but if I were to kneel down, I'd be up to my neck in water."

"Then remain standing, Don Camillo," Christ answered, with a smile.

BIANCO

NOWADAYS THE PEOPLE of the Po River valley go to the city by bus, in one of those cursed modern machines where a human being travels like a trunk, and even if he is sick at his stomach he cannot budge from his seat. And during the winter, when there is a heavy fog or a treacherous coating of ice on the roads, he risks, at the very least, ending up in a ditch.

And to think that once upon a time there was a steam trolley which ran smoothly along its track through fog and ice! Until one fine day a city slicker discovered that the steam trolley was out of date and substituted its fidelity for the fickleness of a vehicle supposedly more modern.

The steam trolley, used to transport not only people, but sand, gravel, bricks, coal, wood, and vegetables as well. It was eminently practical and at the same time full of poetry. Then, one day a dozen workmen wearing municipal badges appeared upon the scene and proceeded to tear up the tracks. And nobody protested; in fact, the general comment was: "It's about time." Because nowadays even old women who go to the city no more than once a year and spend the rest of their time just waiting for time to go by, are in a hurry.

The steam trolley ran from the city to the River, and no farther, although this was not the end of the line. The largest villages of the region are strung out along the highway followed by the trolley, except for a particularly important one, two or three miles away, which the trolley could not have reached except by making a long detour among the canals. On the road which linked this village to the highway, a special horse-drawn car carried passengers to and fro.

Bianco, the last horse to perform this service, was the handsomest of the lot, a beast so noble that he seemed to have stepped down from some public monument. On the village road the ties between the two rails of the trolley line had been covered with tightly packed dirt and along this path Bianco trotted six times a day. A few minutes before the car came to a stop, that is, as soon as he heard the brake grinding, Bianco stepped out from between the rails and trotted alongside them. Then, as soon as the driver called: "Whoa!" he slowed down, without any danger of the car's bumping into his hindquarters.

Bianco was on the job for a number of years and knew it thoroughly. He had extraordinarily keen ears and could hear the trolley's steam whistle long before anyone knew that it was coming. He heard the whistle announcing the trolley's arrival at Trecaselli and pawed the stable floor to signify that it was time to hitch him to his car, pick up the village passengers, and start for the highway, in order to reach it with five minutes to spare. The first day that the whistle failed to sound because the steam trolley was no longer running, Bianco seemed to be bewitched. He stood tensely, with his ears sticking straight up into the air, and waited. For a whole week he behaved the same way, until finally he set his mind at rest.

Yes, Bianco was a fine creature, and when the trolley company put him up at auction everyone wanted to buy him. Barchini was the highest bidder, and he hitched Bianco to a brand-new red wagon. Even between the wagon shafts, Bianco cut a handsome figure. The first time that he was hitched to the wagon, Bianco almost upset his new master, who was sitting on top of a load of beets. For when Barchini called out: "Whoa!" and pulled the reins, Bianco stepped to one side so abruptly that Barchini almost toppled over. But this was the only time that Bianco's memory tricked him; he caught on at once to the fact that the wagon was very different from a car running on rails. He had a touch of nostalgia every time he went along the road between the village and the highway. On the way out, nothing happened, but when he started home Bianco had a way of walking on the extreme left-hand side of the road, beside the ditch where the track had formerly been laid. The years went by, but, as he grew older, Bianco was such a good fellow that Barchini considered him one of the family, and even when he was completely run down no one dreamed of getting rid of him. He was given light work, and one day when Barchini caught a hired man giving him a beating, he got after him with a pitchfork, and if the fellow hadn't run up into the hayloft, he would have found himself speared.

With the passage of the years, Bianco became increasingly weary and indifferent. There came a time when he did not swish his tail to scare off the flies, and he never had to be tied up because there was no likelihood that he would move from the place where anyone left him. He stood stock-still, with his head hanging, like a stuffed horse instead of a real one.

One Saturday afternoon Bianco was hitched to a light cart to take a bag of flour to Don Camillo. While the driver carried the bag into the rectory on his shoulder, Bianco waited outside with his head hanging. All of a sudden he raised his head and pricked up his ears. The sight was so unexpected that Don Camillo, who was standing at the door lighting a cigar, let the match drop from his hand. Bianco stood tautly on the alert for several minutes, and then, wonder of wonders, bolted away. He galloped across the square, and it was sheer luck that nobody was run down. Then he turned into the road leading to the highway and disappeared, leaving a cloud of dust in his wake.

"Bianco's gone crazy," people shouted.

Peppone came by on his motorcycle, and Don Camillo tucked up his cassock and mounted behind him.

"Fast!" Don Camillo shouted, and Peppone threw out the clutch and stepped on the gas.

Bianco galloped down the road, with the cart swaying behind, as if it were tossed on a stormy sea. If it didn't smash to pieces, it must have been because the patron saint of carts had his eye on it. Peppone drove his motorcycle at full speed, and halfway up the road the horse was overtaken.

"Run along beside him," said Don Camillo, "and I'll try to catch the rein near the bit."

Peppone steered close, and Don Camillo stretched out his hand toward the rein. For a moment Bianco seemed to remember that he was a very old nag and consented to being

:[179]:

caught; then suddenly he speeded up and Don Camillo had to let go.

"Let him run!" Don Camillo shouted into Peppone's ear. "Go faster, and we'll wait for him at the highway."

Peppone stepped on the gas, and the motorcycle shot ahead. When they reached the highway, Peppone braked. He tried to say something, but Don Camillo motioned to him to be silent. A few seconds later Bianco galloped into sight. Soon he threatened to join the highway traffic and Peppone had an impulse to give the alarm. But he didn't move in time, and then, after all, it turned out to be unncessary. When Bianco reached the highway he came to a halt and dropped down on one side. He lay there sprawling in the dust, while the cart fell, with its shafts broken, into the ditch. Along the highway came the steam-roller, which was flattening out a coat of macadam. As the steam-roller passed by it whistled and then from the bag of bones—which was all that was left of Bianco —came a whinny. That was the end; now Bianco was a bag of bones indeed. Peppone stood looking down at the carcass, then he tore off his cap and threw it down on the ground.

"Just like the State!" he shouted.

"What do you mean, the State?" asked Don Camillo.

Peppone turned around with a fierce look on his face.

"The State! A man may say he's against it, but when the whistle calls him, he comes forward, and there he is."

"Where is he?" asked Don Camillo.

"Here! There! Everywhere!" shouted Peppone. "With his helmet on his head, his gun in hand and a knapsack over his shoulder . . . And then it turns out that the call came not from the trolley but from a steam-roller. But meanwhile he's a dead duck!"

Peppone wanted to say a great many things, but he didn't know where to begin. He picked up his cap, put it on his head and then lifted it again in salutation.

"A salute to the People!" he exclaimed.

People began to arrive, in carts and on bicycles, and among them was Barchini.

"He heard the whistle of the steam-roller," Don Camillo explained, "and believed it was the trolley. That was plain from the way he stopped at the highway."

Barchini nodded. "The main thing is that he should have died believing," he said.

THE UGLY MADONNA

Don CAMILLO HAD A
thorn in the flesh, one that had annoyed him intensely for a
very long time. Once a year it was particularly painful, and
that was during the procession in honor of the Assumption. For
three hundred and sixty-four days the dim, shadowy chapel
afforded concealment, but under the pitiless sun of August
fifteenth the true state of affairs was visible to everybody. And
it was a serious matter.

She was known as the "ugly Madonna," a phrase which

smacked of collective blasphemy. But actually no disrespect toward the Mother of God was intended; this was merely an accurate description of the statue which was the cause of Don Camillo's pain. The statue was a six-foot-tall terracotta affair, as heavy as lead, and painted in colors so offensive as to give anyone an eyeache. The sculptor—God rest his soul!—must have been one of the most miserable cheats the world has ever known. If an ignorant but honest man had done the job, no one would have called it ugly. Ignorance is not detrimental to a work of art, because a simple-minded craftsman may put his heart and soul into it and these count for infinitely more than his technical ability. But in this case the sculptor was obviously able and had turned all his skill to the creation of something ugly.

On that day long ago when Don Camillo had set foot in the church for the first time, he was shocked by the statue's ugliness and he determined then and there to replace it with some more fitting image of God's Mother. He declared this intention on the spot, and was told to forget it. It was pointed out to him that the statue dated from 1693, and there was a date on the pedestal to prove it.

"I don't care about the date," Don Camillo objected. "It's downright ugly."

"Ugly, but venerably antique," they insisted.

"Venerably antique, but ugly," retorted Don Camillo.

"Historical, Father," they said, insisting upon having the last word.

For several years Don Camillo struggled in vain. If the statue had such historical importance, then it could be sent to a museum and replaced by one with a decent face. Or, if this wouldn't do, it could be moved into the sacristy and thus make way for a more suitable successor. Of course the purchase of another statue would require money. When

:[183]:

Don Camillo started to make the rounds with fund-raising in view, he came upon more opposition.

"Replace the ugly Madonna? That statue is historical, and nothing can take its place. It wouldn't be right. Who ever heard of crowding out history?"

Don Camillo gave the project up, but the statue remained a thorn in his flesh, and every now and then he exploded to Christ at the main altar about it.

"Lord, why don't You help me? Aren't You personally offended by the sight of Your Mother in such an unworthy guise? How can you bear for people to call her the "ugly Madonna?"

"Don Camillo," Christ answered, "true beauty does not reside in the face. That, as we all know, must one day return to the dust from which it sprang. True beauty is eternal and does not die with the flesh. And the beauty of the Mother of God is in her soul and hence incorruptible. Why should I take offense because someone has carved a woman with an ugly face and set her up as a Madonna? Those who kneel before her aren't praying to a statue but to the Mother of God in Heaven."

"Amen," said Don Camillo.

There was no other answer, but it still troubled him to hear people refer to the "ugly Madonna." He became accustomed to the thorn in his flesh, but every August fifteenth, when the statue was taken down and carried in the procession, the pain was more than he could bear. Once removed from the kindly shadows of the chapel and exposed to the sunlight, the face stood out all too clearly. It was not only an ugly face but an evil one as well; the features were heavy and vulgar, and the eyes expressionless rather than ecstatic. And the Infant Jesus in the Madonna's arms was just a bundle of rags with an empty doll's head sticking out of them. Don Camillo had tried to mask the ugliness of the statue with a crown and necklace and veil, but these had served only to accentuate it. Finally he removed all extraneous ornaments and let the vile coloring show for exactly what it was.

Then war came to the river valley, leaving in its wake death and destruction. Bombs fell upon churches and thieving, sacrilegious hands plundered their altars as they passed by. Don Camillo didn't dare admit it but he secretly hoped that someone would "liberate" him from the "ugly Madonna." When foreign soldiers first appeared upon the scene Don Camillo hurried to the proper authorities to say:

"Our ugly Madonna is a masterpiece dating from 1693, an object of both historical and artistic importance. Shouldn't it be evacuated to a safe place of storage for the duration?"

But they told him to set his mind at rest. Historically and artistically important as the Madonna might be, the fact remained that she was ugly, and this was her best defense. If she hadn't been ugly, she would never have stayed in place for so many years.

The war came to an end, and the first post-war years went by, and then a time came when the thorn in Don Camillo's flesh bothered him most acutely. He had painted the church walls, varnished the imitation marble columns and the wooden railings and gilded the candlesticks on the various altars. As a result, the "ugly Madonna" simply didn't belong. A dark spot on a gray background is not too conspicuous, but on a white one it stands out like a black eye.

"Lord," said Don Camillo, on his knees before Christ. "This time You simply must help me. I've spent all the money I had and some I didn't have on fixing up the church. In order to pay my debts, I've rationed my food and given up cigars. And I rejoice not so much in the beauty of the church as in the God-given strength to sacrifice a few of my comforts.

:[185]:

Now, won't You deliver me of the thorn in my flesh? Won't You do something to stop people from calling Don Camillo's church the 'Church of the Ugly Madonna'?"

"Don Camillo, do I have to tell you the same thing over and over?" Christ answered. "Do I have to tell you again that true beauty does not reside in the face, that true beauty cannot be seen, because it is a thing of the spirit, which defies the erosion of time and does not return to the dust whence the body sprang?"

Don Camillo lowered his head without answering. And this was a bad sign.

The feast of the Assumption was drawing near, and one day Don Camillo summoned those who would carry the statue in the procession.

"This year the route followed by the procession will be longer than usual," he told them, "because we must go as far as the newly built houses along the south road."

It was a steaming hot August, and the idea of walking an extra mile over a freshly gravelled road was enough to make even a strong man flinch.

"We might carry the statue in two shifts," suggested old Giarola, who was in charge of arrangements.

"That's dangerous," said Don Camillo. "The sun beats down and 'the bearers' hands get sweaty and may slip just at the moment of changing. No, I think we might rig up Rebecci's small truck. As a matter of fact, that would add to the dignity of the whole thing, and I don't see any real objections."

In a way the bearers were half sorry, but when they thought of the length of the route and the heat of the sun, they felt relieved and gave their assent. Rebecci was glad to lend his truck, and the next day he brought it to the shed back of the rectory. Don Camillo insisted on decorating it in per-

:[186]:

son and for a whole week he worked so hard that all over the village they could hear the sound of his hammer. He had built a platform on the back of the truck and then covered it with draperies and flowers, producing a truly magnificent effect. When Sunday came, the "ugly Madonna" was brought out of the church and hoisted up on to the platform. The pedestal was tied down with strong ropes and these were covered with garlands of flowers.

"You don't have to worry about the driving," Don Camillo said to Rebecci. "Even if you go fifty miles an hour, I guarantee that it will hold fast."

"With all those decorations the Madonna is very nearly beautiful," people said when the truck started.

The procession began to wind its way toward the south road, with the truck moving at the speed of a man's walk. The freshly laid gravel was bumpy and the clutch suddenly got something wrong with it, which jolted the truck so hard that if Don Camillo hadn't tied the pedestal securely to the platform, the "ugly Madonna" would have been out of luck. Don Camillo saw that something was wrong and knew that Rebecci must be worried about it, so when they reached the south road he decided to change the route.

"The truck can't go so slowly over the gravel," he said, "so we'll cut across the fields to the highway. Rebecci will drive back at normal speed and wait for us at the bridge. There we'll re-form the procession and march on a smooth surface all the way back to the center of the village."

Rebecci went dutifully back, and the "ugly Madonna" made the most uncomfortable trip of her long life. The procession re-formed at the bridge and moved smoothly along the paved road, although occasionally Rebecci's clutch caused the truck to leap forward as if someone had given a kick from behind. The village was all decked out, especially the main street, with the arcades on either side, where every house was covered with streamers and people threw handfuls of flowers out the windows. Unfortunately this street was paved with cobble-stones, and because the truck had hard tires as well as a broken clutch, it bounced up and down as if it had St. Vitus dance. But the "ugly Madonna" seemed to be glued to the platform, through Don Camillo's particular merit. Halfway down the main street, however, there was an especially rough bit of paving, punctuated by holes left from the construction of a sewer running below it.

"Once they're over that, there's no more danger," people said. Although they had complete faith in Don Camillo, they left a considerable space between themselves and the bouncing truck.

But the "ugly Madonna" did not get through the danger zone. She didn't fall, because Don Camillo's ropes held her fast, but on a particularly rough bump she just crumbled into pieces. The statue was not made out of terracotta after all; it was some infernal mixture of brick dust or plaster or who knows what, and after two or three thousand death-dealing blows such as it had just received an inevitable fate overtook it. But the shout which rose from the bystanders was not occasioned by the crumbling of the "ugly Madonna." It was a salute to the "fair Madonna," which as if by a miracle took its place.

On the pedestal, which was still roped securely to the truck, there emerged, like a butterfly coming out of its cocoon, a somewhat smaller statue of solid silver. Don Camillo stared at it in astonishment, and into his mind came Christ's words: "True beauty does not reside in the face . . . True beauty cannot be seen, because it is a thing of the spirit, which defies the erosion of time and does not return to the dust whence the body sprang . . ." Then he turned around, because an old woman was shouting:

"A miracle! A miracle!"

He shouted her down and then stooped over to pick up a fragment of the "ugly Madonna," a piece of one of the expressionless eyes which had once so annoyed him.

"We'll put you together again, piece by piece," he said in a loud voice, "even if it takes us ten years; yes, I'll do it myself, you poor 'ugly Madonna' who concealed and saved this silver statue from one of the many barbarian invasions of the last three hundred years. Whoever hurriedly threw you together to cloak the Silver Madonna made you ugly on purpose, so as not to attract an invader already on the march against this village or some distant city from which you may have originally come. When we have put you together, piece by piece, you shall stand side by side with your silver sister. Quite involuntarily, I brought you to this miserable end."

Don Camillo was telling the most shameless lie of his life. But he could not, in the face of his assembled parish, explain that he had chosen a round-about and rocky route for the procession, blown up the truck tires to the bursting-point, sabotaged the clutch and even abetted the destructive power of holes and gravel by driving a pointed tool into the terracotta and starting to crack it open, which last effort he had abandoned when he had seen that the material of which the ugly statue was made would crumble of its own accord. He meant to confess it to Christ, Who of course already knew about it. Meanwhile he went on with his peroration.

"Poor 'ugly Madonna,' you saved the silver statue from one of the many waves of barbarian invaders. But who will save the Silver Madonna from the barbarians of today as they press at our frontiers and eye with hatred the citadel of Christ? Is your appearance an omen? Does it mean that the new barbarians will not invade our valleys, or that if they do, our strong faith and powerful arms will defend you? . . ."

Peppone, who was standing in the front row, in order to "observe the phenomenon more closely," turned to his lieutenant, Smilzo: "What's he mean by the 'new barbarians'?" he asked him.

Smilzo shrugged his shoulders. "Just a bit of unbridled clerical imagination."

There was a moment of silence and then the procession continued.

THE FLYING SQUAD

THAT YEAR AS USUAL, the time came around for "Party Paper Promotion Day." Peppone himself was supposed to go around hawking papers in order to give a good example, but he didn't want to be caught out on a limb and so three or four days beforehand he stopped Don Camillo, who was coming back from a parochial call he had made on his bicycle.

"Once is enough, Father, but twice is too much," Peppone said solemnly.

"What do you mean?" asked Don Camillo, putting one foot on the ground.

"Sunday is Party Paper Promotion Day, and I'm not going to stand any joking. You stick to your business and I'll stick to mine. An insult to me is an insult to the Party."

Don Camillo shook his head.

"If I meet you on the street, I can at least buy a paper, can't I?"

"No, if a reactionary in uniform approaches the local leader of the People's Party to buy the People's Party paper, it's an attempt to provoke violence. It's almost as bad as if I were to force a paper on you. Each one of us should stick to his own job: you dish out propaganda for the Pope and I dish it out for the Party."

"Good," said Don Camillo. "Then you admit that dishing out propaganda for the Pope is within my rights."

"Of course, as long as you don't do it in an aggressive and provocative fashion. Within your own province you can dish out propaganda for anything you damn please."

"That's a bargain!"

When Sunday morning came, Peppone had mapped out his strategy.

"We won't show our faces, because rather than buy a paper these people are capable of staying away from Mass. Of course, their staying away is a Party triumph, because it rescues them for once from the domination of the clergy. But the Party paper doesn't profit. We'll spread word that we've gone to Castelletto and that way they'll be tricked into going to Mass. When they all come out at noon, we'll blockade the square and see who has the nerve to refuse the paper!"

The plan worked well. People went to Mass, and a few minutes before noon every street leading away from the square was covered. But when twelve o'clock came nobody left the church.

"He's caught on to the trick and is dragging out the Mass so as to keep them there longer," said Peppone. "But a lot of good that will do him!"

A few minutes later, they did pour out, but instead of scattering they stood compactly together.

"What are those devils up to?" mumbled Peppone. "They must be waiting for someone."

Just then there came a loud noise from the top of the church tower.

"He's set up a loud-speaker," Peppone shouted. "But if he makes a political speech there'll be hell to pay."

The noise from the loud-speaker increased, and became recognizable as the applause of a crowd. Then came a clear, powerful voice, that of the Pope speaking to two hundred and fifty thousand citizens of Rome. He spoke succinctly of the cardinal imprisoned by the Reds of Hungary, and when the loud-speaker had spilled the last wave of shouting and cheering down from the church tower, the village square was filled with people. They had come out of their houses, even the oldest and most infirm among them, from every direction, and Peppone's gang was disrupted and drowned in their surge. Some people were hurrying home, others talking excitedly to one another and feeling braced up by the two hundred and fifty thousand Romans gathered in St. Peter's Square. When the unexpected broadcast from Rome was over, Don Camillo turned on the gramophone, and a flood of music and singing kept the villagers' spirits high.

In the end, Peppone's gang found themselves still holding their papers in the middle of a deserted square. Smilzo tried offering them to a few stragglers, but they paid him no attention. Peppone was the last one to regain his self-control. He had such confusion in his head and such convulsions of rage in his stomach that he didn't know whether he was coming or going. He began to see straight only when Don

Camillo appeared at the church's open door. With lowered head, Peppone advanced toward him, and when he had come close he stood his ground and clenched his teeth. Don Camillo looked at him with a smile.

"As you see, I kept my part of our bargain," he said. "You advertised the Party and I advertised the Pope."

When you have a whole dictionary full of swear-words in your mind, it is useless to even begin to come out with them, so Peppone merely drew a sigh that had the volume of a cyclone. He stood there, with lowered head, wishing that he had horns like a bull and could disembowel Don Camillo and the whole of Christianity as well.

"Give me a copy of your paper," said a voice, and fifteen liras floated into Peppone's field of vision. Mechanically he held out the paper and took the money, but before slipping it into his pocket he remembered something, raised his head and saw Don Camillo standing there with the communist paper in his hand. Then he really lost control. He raised the pile of papers above his head and threw them down to the ground with every ounce of strength the Creator had put into his muscles. It was a lovely crash. Then he wheeled about and walked away, while Smilzo picked up the papers and started to follow. But after he had gone a few feet, he turned to throw over his shoulder:

"When Stalin speaks from St. Peter's Square, then you'll hear something!"

Don Camillo showed considerable interest.

"Does your paper say when that's going to be?" he asked.

"No, it doesn't," Smilzo grudgingly admitted.

"Well, for a Russian paper, it's singularly ill informed," Don Camillo said in a loud voice.

Peppone heard him, and wheeling about again he came back and stood in front of Don Camillo.

"Does the Vatican news sheet say when the Pope will speak in Moscow's Red Square?" he asked him.

"No," said Don Camillo.

"Then we're even," Peppone shouted.

Don Camillo threw out his arms in mock despair.

"If that's so, why do you lose your temper so easily?" he asked.

"Because it's not so. And I'd like to see you and that Pope of yours hanging up there where you put the loud-speaker."

"Peppone, you know His Holiness can't travel so far from Rome."

"Then I'll take you there," shouted Peppone. "All I want is to see you swinging from the same gallows."

"You pay me too much honor, Peppone. I'm tempted to buy another copy of your informative paper."

At that Peppone walked away. He had a family and couldn't afford to get into real trouble.

It was a stormy February evening and the valley was full of melancholy and mud. Don Camillo was sitting in front of the fire, looking at some old newspapers, when he got news that something serious had happened. He threw down the papers, put on his black coat and hurried into the church.

"Lord," he said, "there's more trouble with that devil's son."

"Whose son do you mean?" Christ asked.

"Peppone's. God the Father must have it in for him . . ."

"How do you know, Don Camillo? Does God let you look into His books? And how can you intimate that He loves one human being less than another? God is the same for all men."

Don Camillo went behind the altar to search for something in a cabinet.

"Lord, I don't know anything," he said. "The fact is that

:[195]:

Peppone's little boy is badly hurt and they've called me to give him Extreme Unction. A rusty nail did it . . . apparently just a trifle . . . And now he's at death's door."

Having found what he was searching for, Don Camillo passed hastily in front of the altar, genuflected and started to hurry away. But he had only gone half the length of the church when he stopped and came back.

"Lord," he said, when he came to the altar, "I have a lot to say, but no time to say it. I'll explain to You along the way. Meanwhile I'm not taking the Holy Oil with me. I'm leaving it here on the railing."

He walked hurriedly through the rain, and only when he arrived at Peppone's door did he realize that he was holding his hat in his hand. He wiped his head with his coat and knocked. The door opened and a woman led him down the hall. She stopped in front of a door to whisper to him. The door was thrown open with a loud shout, and there was Peppone. Peppone's eyes were startled and bloodshot, and he raised his fists threateningly.

"Get out of here!" he shouted. "Go away!"

Don Camillo did not move. Peppone's wife and his mother were hanging on to him, but Peppone seemed half mad and threw himself upon Don Camillo, grabbing hold of his chest.

"Get out! What do you want here? Did you come to liquidate him? Get out, or I'll strangle you!"

He shouted an oath strong enough to make the sky tremble, but Don Camillo did not blench. Pushing Peppone aside, he walked into the child's room.

"No!" shouted Peppone. "No Holy Oil! If you give him that it means he's done for."

"What Holy Oil are you talking about? I didn't bring any Holy Oil with me."

"Do you swear it?"

"I swear."

Then Peppone grew calm.

"You mean you really didn't bring the Holy Oil?"

"No, why should I?"

Peppone looked at the doctor, then at Don Camillo and then at the child.

"What is the trouble?" Don Camillo asked the doctor.

"Father," the doctor answered, "only streptomycin can save him."

Don Camillo clenched his fists.

"Only streptomycin?" he shouted. "And what about God. Can't God do anything?"

The doctor shrugged his shoulders.

"I'm not a priest, I'm a doctor."

"I'm disgusted with you," said Don Camillo.

"Good," chimed in Peppone.

"And where is this streptomycin?" Don Camillo asked, beside himself.

"In the city," the doctor answered.

"Then we'll go get it."

"It's too late, Father. It's only a matter of minutes now. And there's no way of reaching the city. The telephone and the telegraph are both cut off on account of the storm. There's nothing we can do."

Don Camillo picked up the little boy and wrapped him in a blanket with a rubber sheet over it.

"Come on, you idiot," he shouted to Peppone. "Call out your squad!"

The squad was waiting in Peppone's workshop. It consisted for the moment of Smilzo and a few young loafers.

"There are half a dozen motorcycles in the village. I'll get Breschi's racer, and you round up the rest. If they won't give them to you, shoot."

Then all of them went off in various directions.

"If you don't lend me your motorcycle, this child is going

:[197]:

to die," Don Camillo said to Breschi. "And if he dies, I'll wring your neck."

Breschi was speechless, although deep-down inside he wept at the idea of his brand-new machine being knocked about on a wet night. Ten minutes later the motorcycle squad was complete. A few of the owners had taken a beating, but Don Camillo said that didn't matter.

"With six of us starting, surely one will get to the city," said Don Camillo. He himself was astride the shiny red racer and held the child to him under his coat.

Two ahead, two behind, with Don Camillo in the middle and Peppone out ahead of them all on Brusco's big motorcycle, this was the formation of the "flying squad" as it shot along the deserted valley roads under the rain. The roads were slippery and every curve an unexpected menace. Skirting hedges and ditches, the "flying squad" went through gravel and mud to the paved highway. There the motors began to roar, and they raced in dead earnest. All of a sudden Don Camillo heard a pitiful moan from the bundle he was pressing to him. He must go even faster.

"Lord," he implored through clenched teeth, "give me more gas! And you, you filthy machine, let's see if you have any real guts in you!" The racer seemed to leap ahead, passing all the rest, including Peppone, who didn't have Don Camillo's Lord to give him more gas!

Don Camillo could not remember the details of his arrival. They told him that he charged in with a child in his arms, took the hospital doorman by the neck, thrust a door open with one shoulder and threatened to strangle a doctor. The "flying squad" went home leaving Peppone's boy in the hospital to recover. That same night Don Camillo returned to the village blowing his horns full blast and covered with glorious mud.

HORSES OF A DIFFERENT COLOR

They called him Romagnolo, simply because he came from the province of Romagna. He had come to the village years ago, but he was still *romagnolo* to the core. And to explain what this means I must tell you that this man had the nickname of "Civil-and-with-the-band." In the course of a political rally, the platform under him gave way and he started to fall to the ground. Upon which he called out with alacrity: "Civil, and with the band!" to signify that he wanted a civil burial, and not a church one, with the band playing the Hymn of Garibaldi in slow tempo for a funeral march. When they start a new town in Romagna, they first throw up a monument to Garibaldi and then build a church, because there's no fun in a civil funeral unless it spites the parish priest. The whole history of the province is concerned with spite of this kind.

Now Romagnolo was a man with the gift of gab and one who spoke with the big words that can be read in revolutionary papers. The fact that there was no more king had knocked the props from under his pet subject for an argument, so he had to concentrate his heavy artillery upon the clergy. He finished every speech with the sentence:

"When I die, I want a civil funeral and the band playing."

Don Camillo was acquainted with the whole story, but had never paid it any attention. And so one day Romagnolo buttonholed him in order to say:

"For your information, remember that after having steered clear of you my whole life long, I intend to steer clear of you when I'm dead. I don't want any priest at my funeral."

"Very well," said Don Camillo calmly. "Only you're barking up the wrong tree. You ought to go to the veterinary. I look after Christian souls, not animals."

Romagnolo started to make a speech.

"When that Pope of yours . . ."

"Don't bother anyone so far away. Let's stick to present company. I'll have to pray God to grant you a long life so that you'll have plenty of time to think better of it."

When Romagnolo celebrated his ninetieth birthday the whole village turned out for the festivities, including Don Camillo, who walked up to him with a smile and said: "Congratulations!"

Romagnolo shot him a resentful look and shouted:

"You'd better pray to your God again. Some day or other He'll have to let me die. And then it will be my turn to laugh."

The strange business of the horses took place in the following year.

The business of the horses took place in a village on the other side of the river.

A seventy-four year old Red had died, and they held a civil funeral, with red flags, red carnations, red kerchiefs, and in short red everything. The coffin was placed on the hearse carriage, the band began to play the song "Red Flag," in funereal tempo, and the horses started forward with their heads hanging low as they always did on such occasions. Behind them came the procession, with red flags flying. But when they reached the church, the horses came to a stop and no one could make them budge. Several men pulled them by their bridles and others pushed the hearse from behind, but the horses stood their ground. When someone took a whip and began to beat them over the back, the horses reared up and then fell onto their knees. Finally they were set on their feet and walked along for a short distance, but when they got to the cemetery they reared up again and started to go backward.

The old man himself hadn't refused to have a religious funeral, the newspapers explained; his sons had imposed their ideas upon him. The story travelled all over the countryside, and anyone who wanted to test the truth of it had only to cross the river to hear it first-hand. Whenever a little knot of people gathered to discuss it, Romagnolo would descend upon them, shouting: "Middle Ages. That's stuff for the Middle Ages!"

And he went on to say that there was nothing miraculous about it; there was a perfectly rational explanation. For years immemorial the horses had stopped in front of the church, and so they had followed their usual habit this time as well. People were impressed by this version of the story and went to Don Camillo about it.

"What do you say?"

Don Camillo threw out his arms.

"Divine Providence knows no limits, and may well choose the humblest flower or tree or stone to teach a lesson to men. The sad part of it is that men pay so little attention to those of their fellows whose job it is to explain God's word, and choose rather to heed the example given them by a horse or a dog."

Many people were disappointed with this way of speaking and some of Don Camillo's most important parishioners brought their complaints to the rectory.

"Father, this thing has created quite a sensation. Instead of dismissing it so lightly, you ought to interpret it and bring out its moral teaching."

"I can't say anything more than what I said before," answered Don Camillo. "When God decided to give men the Ten Commandments he did it, not through a horse, but through a man. Do you think that God is so badly off as to call upon horses? You know the facts; let each one of you take from them what lesson he may. If you don't like what I have said, go to the bishop and tell him to put a horse in my place."

Meanwhile Romagnolo was sputtering with rage, because people shrugged their shoulders at his explanation.

"That's all very well," they said, "there's nothing extraordinary or miraculous involved, but . . ."

So it was that Romagnolo buttonholed Don Camillo again.

"Father, you're just the man I wanted to see. What is the official interpretation of the horse story?"

"Barking up the wrong tree, as usual," Don Camillo replied with a smile. "Horses aren't my line. You ought to go to the veterinary."

Romagnolo made a long speech to explain the horses' behavior, and at the end Don Camillo simply threw out his arms.

"I can see that the thing has made quite an impression upon you. If it has caused you to stop and think, then I say thank God for it."

Romagnolo raised a threatening, skinny finger.

"I can tell you one thing," he said, "and that is, the horses won't stop when my coffin passes by!"

Don Camillo went to talk to Christ on the altar.

"Lord, the foolish things he says are not meant to hurt You; they're just barbs directed at me. When he comes up for Judgment, remember that he hails from Romagna. The trouble is that he's over ninety, and anyone could knock him over with a feather. If he were in his prime, it would be a different matter. I'd get after him."

"Don Camillo, the system of teaching Christian charity by knocking people over the head is one that doesn't appeal to me," Christ answered severely.

"I don't approve of it myself," said Don Camillo humbly. "But the fact is that often the ideas people have in their heads aren't so bad; it's just that they're in bad order. And sometimes a good shaking-up will cause them to fall into place."

Romagnolo went to Peppone's office and declared with no preamble: "Take this piece of legal paper, call two of your jumping-jacks to bear witness, and write down what I say."

He threw the piece of paper on the mayor's desk and sat down.

"Put the date on top and write clearly: 'I, the undersigned Libero Martelli, ninety-one years old, by profession a free-thinker, in full possession of all my faculties, desire that upon my death all my property and possessions be transferred to this township for the purpose of buying a motor hearse to take the place of the present horse-drawn vehicle . . .'"

Peppone stopped writing.

"Well?" said Romagnolo. "Do you want me to leave all my worldly goods to the priest?"

"I accept, of course," Peppone stuttered. "But how are we to buy a motor hearse so soon? It would cost at least a million and a half liras, and we . . ."

"I have two millions in the bank. Just go ahead and buy it, and I'll pay."

Romagnolo came out of the town hall glowing with satisfaction and for the first time in his life went deliberately to the church square.

"Everything's settled, Father!" he shouted. "When I go by in my coffin, the horses won't stop. I've taken care of priests and horses alike."

Romagnolo got too excited, and drank more than was good for him. Not that wine did him in, after having been good for him all his life long. Water was his downfall. Coming home one night, full to the gills with wine, he was so overpoweringly sleepy that he lay down in a ditch. At over ninety years of age, spending the night in a puddle of a water isn't exactly healthy. Romagnolo caught pneumonia and died. But before closing his eyes he summoned Peppone.

"Is everything agreed?" he asked him.

"Yes. Your wishes will be faithfully observed."

Romagnolo was the motor hearse's first customer. And the whole village turned out to see its inauguration. The band struck up, and the hearse moved slowly and steadily along. But in front of the church it came to a sudden stop. The driver wriggled the gear lever frantically, but all in vain. He looked under the hood, but found the spark plugs, carburetor and points all in perfect order and the tank full of gasoline. The church door was closed, but Don Camillo was looking through a crack. He saw men milling about the hearse, and the hearse standing, obviously stuck, among them. The band had stopped playing and the bystanders had fallen into an astonished silence. The minutes dragged by, until Don Camillo ran to the sacristy and pulled the bell rope.

"God have mercy on you," he panted; "God have mercy on you . . ."

And the bells tolled out in the silent air. People shook themselves and the driver shifted the gear. The motor started and the motor hearse pulled away. No one could follow it any longer, because the driver put it into second and then into third gear, and it disappeared in a cloud of dust in the direction of the cemetery.

BLUE SUNDAY

O LD MAN GROLINI TURNED
up at the rectory to show Don Camillo a letter. Under the
watchful eye of his dog, Thunder, Don Camillo was greasing
cartridges for his shotgun. Even before he read the letter he
threw a questioning look at Grolini.

"The usual thing," Grolini sputtered. "That little wretch
is in hot water again."

The headmaster of young Grolini's boarding-school was
thoroughly dissatisfied with him and wanted his father to do
something about it.

"You'd better go in my place," Grolini said. "If I go, I'm likely to hit him over the head. When you see him, Father, tell him that if he doesn't behave I'll kick him out of the house."

Don Camillo shook his head.

"That would be even more stupid than hitting him over the head," he muttered. "How can anyone kick a boy out of the house when he's only eleven years old?"

"If I can't kick him out of the house, then I'll send him to the reformatory," shouted Grolini. "I don't want to see him again!"

Seeing that the father was not to be appeased, Don Camillo finally said: "I'll go talk to him Sunday afternoon."

"Then I authorize you to kick him about the school grounds," Grolini shouted. "The worse you treat him the better pleased I'll be."

After Grolini had gone, Don Camillo turned the letter over and over in his hands. The matter troubled him, because he had been the one to advise Grolini to encourage the boy in his studies and send him away to school. Grolini was a rich man. He tilled the soil, but the soil was his own. It was fertile soil, to boot, and he had livestock in his stable and as many tractors and other agricultural machines as he could desire. Giacomino, his youngest son, was a quick-witted fellow, who had always done well at school, and his father was attracted by the idea of having a university graduate in the family. Not to mention his wife, who gave herself very great airs. So it was that as soon as Giacomino had finished elementary school he was bundled off to the city. Don Camillo had filled out his application papers and escorted him there in person. Giacomino was one of the mildest and best boys Don Camillo had ever known. He had been an acolyte for years and never got himself into the least trouble. So now the priest could not understand why he had turned out so badly.

When Sunday came, Don Camillo appeared at the boarding-school at the visitors' hour. When the headmaster heard the name of Grolini he held his head in his hands. Don Camillo threw out his arms in a gesture of hopelessness.

"I'm amazed," he said with mortification. "I always knew him to be a good, obedient boy. I can't understand why he should be so wild."

" 'Wild' isn't exactly the word for it," the headmaster put in. "His conduct doesn't give us any worry. But we're more concerned about him than about the worst boys in the school."

He took an envelope out of his desk drawer and drew forth a sheet of paper.

"Look at this composition," he said.

Don Camillo found himself looking at a clean paper, bearing on it in neat writing: *Giacomo Grolini. Class IB. Theme: My favorite book. Exposition.*

Turning the page, he came upon a perfect blank.

"There you are," said the headmaster, holding out the entire envelope to him. "All his class work follows the same pattern. He neatly puts down the theme subject or problem, then sits back with folded arms and waits for the time to go by. When he's asked a question, he makes no answer. First we thought he must be a perfect idiot. But we've watched him and listened to him talk to his companions, and we find he isn't an idiot at all. Quite the contrary."

"I'll talk to him," said Don Camillo. "I'll take him to some quiet place outside, and if necessary, I'll give him a proper dressing-down."

The headmaster looked at Don Camillo's big hands.

"If you can't bring him around that way, I'm afraid there's

nothing more to do," he mumbled. "He has no right to leave the premises after the way he's behaved, but I'll give him permission to stay out with you until five o'clock."

When Giacomino arrived on the scene a few minutes later, Don Camillo did not even recognize him. Quite aside from his school uniform and closely clipped hair, there was something entirely new in his manner.

"Have no fear," Don Camillo said to the headmaster. "I'll work on him."

They walked in silence through the empty streets, typical of a tedious Sunday afternoon, and beside the bulky priest, Giacomino looked smaller and skinnier than ever. When they had reached the outskirts, Don Camillo looked around for a place where they could talk freely. He turned onto a thoroughfare leading out into the country and then fifty yards later onto a dirt road running along a canal. The sun was shining, and although the trees were bare, the landscape was pleasant to the eye. Finally Don Camillo sat down on a tree trunk. He had in mind the speech he intended to make to the boy, and it was ferocious enough to make an elephant quiver. Giacomino stood in front of him and suddenly said:

"May I have a run?"

"A run?" said Don Camillo severely. "Can't you run during recreation at school?"

"Yes, but not very far," the boy answered. "There's always a wall in the way."

Don Camillo looked at the boy's pale face and clipped hair.

"Have your run, then," he said, "and then come here. I want to talk to you."

Giacomino was off like a bolt of lightning, and Don Camillo saw him cross the field, duck under a fence and run parallel to it under some bare grapevines. A few minutes later he came back, with his eyes and cheeks glowing.

"Rest a minute and then we'll talk," mumbled Don Camillo.

The boy sat down, but a minute later he jumped to his feet and ran over to an elm near by. He climbed it like a squirrel and made for a vine among its top branches. He explored among the red leaves and then came down with something in his hand.

"Grapes!" he exclaimed to Don Camillo, showing him a cluster that had survived the Fall picking. He proceeded to eat the grapes one by one and when he had finished he sat down beside the trunk.

"May I throw a stone?" he asked.

Don Camillo continued to lie low. "Go ahead and amuse yourself," he was thinking, "and we'll talk business later."

The boy rose, picked up a stone, brushed the dirt off it and threw it with all his strength. Don Camillo had a feeling that the stone had flown behind the clouds, never to return. A cold wind had blown up, and Don Camillo began to think they had better repair to some quiet café, where he wouldn't have to shout in order to make the boy hear him. As they walked away, Giacomino asked permission to race ahead and found another cluster of grapes left from the Fall.

"That's just a small part of what there must have been on the vine!" he murmured as he ate them. "At home now, they must have hung up the grapes to dry . . ."

"Never mind about the grapes," Don Camillo mumbled.

The outskirts of the city were squalid and melancholy. As they walked along they met a man selling roast chestnuts and peanuts. Giacomino opened his eyes wide.

"Silly stuff," said Don Camillo ill-humoredly. "I'll get you a piece of cake when we sit down."

"No thanks," said the boy, in a tone of voice that set Don Camillo's nerves on edge.

The nut vendor knew his business and had stopped a few

yards back of them. And the proof of his astuteness was that Don Camillo turned around and grudgingly tossed him a hundred-lira note.

"Mixed, Father?"

"Yes, mixed."

Don Camillo put the bag of silly stuff into the boy's hand, and they continued to walk along the deserted thoroughfare. The priest held out as long as he could, and then finally stuck his hand into the bag. The taste of the nuts called up memories of the melancholy Sunday afternoons of his own youth, and filled him with a sudden sadness. A church bell rang, and when Don Camillo pulled out his heavy gold watch he saw that it was twenty minutes to five.

"Hurry," he said to the boy. "You must be back promptly on the hour."

They quickened their pace, as the sun sank below the houses around them. When they arrived, without a minute to spare, the boy held the bag out to Don Camillo.

"When you come back from outside they take everything like this away," he explained in a low voice.

Don Camillo put the bag into his pocket.

"That's where I sleep," said the boy, pointing to a barred second-storey window with a box-like protuberance under it that blocked the sight of the ground below. Then he hesitated for a moment before pointing to a window on the ground floor, barred in the same way but affording a view of the world outside.

"In that hall are the closets where we hang our clothes," he said. "I'll try to walk along it on my way upstairs and that way I'll be able to wave goodbye."

Don Camillo went with him to the heavy front door, then he came back and waited on the sidewalk outside the ground-floor window, which gave onto a side street. Nervously he lit a cigar. After what seemed like an endless time, he heard a whisper. Giacomino had opened a window and was waving to him from behind the bars. Don Camillo walked over and handed him the bag of nuts. Then he started to walk away, but something made him turn back. He could see nothing of Giacomino but a pair of eyes, but these were so filled with tears that Don Camillo broke out into a cold perspiration. By some mysterious process his dangerously powerful hands found themselves twisting the iron bars and the iron bars bent and gave way. When the opening was large enough, Don Camillo stretched out an arm, grasped the boy's collar and pulled him through. It was dark by now, and no one saw anything strange in the sight of a priest and a schoolboy walking together.

"Wait for me," Don Camillo said, "while I get my motorcycle out of the lot."

By eight o'clock they were back in the village, and Giacomino had eaten all the nuts on the way.

"Come into the rectory by the back door," Don Camillo told him as they got off the motorcycle, "and don't let anyone see you."

By nine o'clock Giacomino was sleeping on a couch in the hall while Don Camillo finished his supper in the kitchen. At a quarter past nine Grolini turned up, waving a telegram in one hand.

"That rascal has run away from school," he shouted. "If I lay my hands on him, I'll kill him for sure."

"Then I hope you don't lay hands on him," Don Camillo murmured.

Grolini was beside himself with anger.

"At least you gave him one good scolding this afternoon," he added.

Don Camillo shook his head.

"Nothing doing. That boy was made to follow in your footsteps and live on the land. He simply can't stay away from the country. A good little fellow, too . . . But perhaps he's dead by now."

"Dead?" Grolini shouted.

Don Camillo sighed.

"I found him in a very bad state of mind, and he talked to me in a most alarming way . . . You'd more or less given him up for lost, hadn't you? I told him what you said, that rather than see his face again you'd send him to the reformatory."

Grolini sank onto a chair and finally managed to say:

"Father, if God brings him home safe and sound I'll foot the bill for repairs to the bell tower."

"That's not necessary," said Don Camillo gently. "God will be satisfied with your grief. Go back home, and don't lose heart. I'll go look for your boy."

Giacomino came home the next day, and Don Camillo was with him. His family were gathered in the yard, but no one said a word. Only Flick, the old dog, barked and jumped like a kangaroo because he was so happy. Giacomino threw him his school cap and Flick ran off, holding it between his teeth with Giacomino running after him.

"The headmaster called me up this morning," said old man Grolini. "He can't understand how the boy could have twisted two heavy iron bars."

"He's an able boy, I tell you," said Don Camillo. "He'll make a very good farmer. And it's better to farm for love than to study for fear of a beating."

And Don Camillo went away very fast, because he had just felt a peanut in his pocket and couldn't wait to eat it.

DON CAMILLO
GETS IN TROUBLE

SAINT MARTIN'S SUMMER
brought some strangers to the village, among them a certain
Marasca, who might better have stayed away. Marasca had a
little boy and when he took him for the first time to school he
said to the teacher:

"I hear that the priest comes every Wednesday to give
religious instruction. When he arrives, will you kindly send
my boy home?"

And since the teacher told him that was impossible, every

Wednesday Marasca kept the boy out of school. Don Camillo stayed out of it as long as he could, then one Wednesday afternoon he went to Olmetto, the farm where Marasca was a tenant. He meant to make a joke of it rather than to stir up trouble, but at first sight Marasca showed signs of not appreciating his visit.

"This is my land," he said. "You must have crossed the wrong bridge."

"No, I didn't cross the wrong bridge," said Don Camillo. "I hear that on Wednesdays your boy can't come to school, and so I thought I'd give him a little religious instruction at home."

Marasca came out with an oath that was really more than Don Camillo deserved.

"I see you need a little religious instruction yourself," said the priest, "and I'm ready to give it to you."

Marasca's brother came out of the house and looked threateningly at the visitor.

"Get out of here and don't let me see you again, you cursed black crow!" shouted Marasca.

Don Camillo did not say a word. He retraced his steps, and when he was across the bridge and back on the road, he called out:

"Now I'm off your land," he said. "But you'll have to come repeat what you just said, because I didn't understand."

The two brothers looked at one another; then they crossed the bridge and planted themselves defiantly in front of Don Camillo. And there they found that the priest had quite a bag of tricks up his sleeve. While he was slapping the dust off the face of the first Marasca, the brother, who had already had a taste of the same medicine, ran back to the yard and returned with a pitchfork. The pitchfork was of an ordinary kind, and had a handle. But this was where the trouble began, for in Don Camillo's powerful hands, the handle turned into a regular earthquake. The two Marascas found this out to their sorrow, because the handle was broken on their backs.

The whole village was turned upside down, and the Communist newspaper sent a special correspondent who painted Don Camillo as a dangerously aggressive and violent man. As a result, Don Camillo was called up before the old Bishop, and before he could say any more than: "Self-defense . . ." the bishop interrupted him gently.

"Monterana is without a priest. Go up there this evening and stay until the return of the regular incumbent."

"But the regular incumbent is dead," Don Camillo stammered.

"Exactly," said the Bishop, making a gesture which indicated that he had nothing more to say.

Don Camillo bowed his head and went to pack his bag.

Monterana was one of the most forsaken spots on the surface of the globe: half a dozen huts made of mud and stones, one of which was the church, but distinguishable from the others only because of the bell tower at its side. The road to Monterana was a stony ditch, called by courtesy a mule-track, but no mule would ever have ventured upon it. Don Camillo arrived at the top with his heart in his throat and gazed around. When he went into the rectory the walls were so low that they seemed to crush him. A scrawny old woman came out of a hole and looked at him through half-open eyes.

"Who are you?" Don Camillo asked, but she threw out her arms as if to say that she had forgotten.

The main beam of the kitchen ceiling was supported by a tree trunk in the middle of the room, and Don Camillo was tempted to play the part of Sampson and pull the whole place down around him. Then he realized that another priest, a man like himself, had spent a lifetime amid these same squalid surroundings, and this caused him to recover some of his calm. He went into the church, and the miserable condition of it brought tears to his eyes. He knelt on the step before the altar and raised his eyes to the cross.

"Lord . . ." he began, and then he stopped, because the cross was of crudely cut wood, black and peeling; it was completely bare. Don Camillo felt very nearly afraid. "Lord," he sorrowfully exclaimed, "You are everywhere in the universe, and I need no image of You to tell me that You are near, but here I feel as if You had abandoned me . . . My faith must be a very poor thing, if I feel so terribly alone."

He went back to the rectory and there he found a cloth on the table, a loaf of bread and a piece of cheese. The old woman was just bringing in a jug of water.

"Where did these things come from?" Don Camillo asked.
She threw out her arms and looked up to Heaven. Plainly, she didn't know. With the old priest it had always been this way, and now the miracle was repeating itself. Don Camillo made the sign of the cross, and involuntarily thought of the bare, black wooden cross he had just seen on the altar. He shivered, and reproached himself for being afraid. But instead he had a fever, sent to him by Divine Providence, like the bread and the cheese and the water. He stayed in bed for three days, and on the fourth day he received written orders from the Bishop.

"You are not to leave your new post, for any reason whatsoever. Don't show your face in the village, for the people there must forget that they ever had a priest so unworthy. May God strengthen and protect you . . ."

Don Camillo got up, with his head still reeling. He went over to the window and found that it was chilly outside with a premonition of fog in the air.

"Winter will be here any minute," he said to himself with error, "and I shall be snowbound and all alone . . ."

It was five o'clock in the afternoon, and he must not let night overtake him. He rolled rather than walked down the mule-track and reached the road just in time to catch a bus to the city. There he went to several garages, until he found someone who would take him by car to the crossroad at Gaggiola. From the crossroad, Don Camillo cut over the fields and at ten o'clock he was in Peppone's garden.

Peppone stared at him with a worried air.

"I must transport some things to Monterana," said Don Camillo. "Can I hire your truck?"

Peppone shrugged his shoulders.

"Did you have to wake me up for that?" he asked. "We can discuss that tomorrow morning."

"We're going to discuss it right away," the priest insisted. "I need your truck tonight."

"Are you mad?" Peppone asked him.

"Yes," Don Camillo answered.

Upon receiving such a logical reply, Peppone could only scratch his head.

"Let's hurry," said Don Camillo. "How much will it cost?"

Peppone took the stub of a pencil and made some calculations.

"Forty miles there and forty miles back, that makes eighty. Sixty-five hundred liras worth of gasoline and oil. Then there's the charge for my services, which are higher paid at night. But since it's to help you get out of this village, and I'm happy to see you go . . ."

"Come on," said Don Camillo. "How much is it?"

"Ten thousand for the whole job."

Don Camillo agreed, and Peppone stretched out his hand.

"Cash will do it," he muttered.

Ten thousand liras represented Don Camillo's savings of years.

"Get your truck going, and meet me halfway down the Boschetto road."

"What in Heaven's name can you be loading there?"

"That's none of your business, and keep your trap shut."

Peppone muttered something to the effect that in the woods at midnight he probably wouldn't find many people with whom to exchange conversation. Don Camillo's fever excited rather than tired him. He made a detour through the fields and approached the church from the orchard. Or rather he bumped straight into it, because there was thick fog all around. He had his keys in his pocket and went in by the tower door. He had to go out the main entrance, but no one saw him.

Peppone had a bright idea. When he saw the fog and thought of Don Camillo trying to make his way through it with all his bags and baggage, he decided to blow his horn to guide him. Led by the horn and the excitement of his fever, Don Camillo arrived panting at the meeting-place. Peppone started to get down from the truck to help him, but the priest said:

"I don't need any help. Start up your motor and be ready to go when I give the word."

When he had loaded everything on the truck, Don Camillo went to sit beside Peppone, and off they went. The fog pursued them for the first twenty miles, but they made the second half of the trip as fast as if they were flying. At two o'clock in the morning Peppone brought his truck to a halt at the beginning of the famous mule-track leading to Monterana. Don Camillo once more refused Peppone's help in unloading. Peppone heard him scuffling about at the back of the truck and then, when he saw him in the glare of the headlights, his eyes opened wide.

"The Crucified Christ from the altar!"

Don Camillo started the painful ascent of the mule-track, and Peppone had pity and overtook him.

"Father, can I give you a hand?"

"Hands off!" shouted Don Camillo. "Go home, and think twice before you spread any gossip!"

"Here's wishing you a safe arrival!" said Peppone.

And so it was that Don Camillo's Stations of the Cross began.

The crucifix was large and heavy, made out of solid oak. And the figure of the Crucified Christ was carved out of equally heavy, hard wood. The mule-track was steep and its stony surface was bathed by the rain. Never had Don Camillo carried such a weight on his shoulders. His bones creaked, and after half an hour he had to drag the crucifix. The crucifix became heavier and heavier and Don Camillo was more and more tired, but still he did not give up. He slipped and fell on a sharp stone, and felt the blood trickling down from one knee, but still he did not stop. A branch carried away his hat and scratched his forehead, thorns ripped his cassock, but on he climbed, with his face bent low, near to that of the Crucified Christ. Even a gushing spring did not tempt him to linger. One, two, three hours went by.

It took him four hours to reach the village. The church was the building farthest away, and to reach it, he had to climb up a path which was less rocky, but filled with mud. Everyone was still in bed and he made it quite alone, borne up by the hope that is born of despair. He entered the empty church, but his task was not yet over. He still had to dismount the bare, black cross and install his own crucifix on the altar. After one last struggle, his mission was accomplished. Then he collapsed on the floor. But when the bell rang he jumped up, went to wash his hands in the sacristy and said his first Mass. He lit the candles himself; there were only two of them, but they seemed to shed a very great light.

Only two people came to Mass, but Don Camillo had the

sensation of a multitude, because one of the two was the old woman who had forgotten her name. And the other was Peppone, who had been too tired to drive back his truck and had followed Don Camillo step by step up the mountain. Although he did not have the cross on his shoulders, he had felt the priest's weariness as if it were his own. As he went by the poor-box in the church he slipped into it the ten-thousand lira note given him by Don Camillo.

"Lord," whispered Don Camillo, raising his eyes to the Crucified Christ. "I hope you don't mind my having brought You to this wretched place."

"No, Don Camillo," said Christ with a smile. "The place is marvellous."

WHEN THE RAINS CAME

Everyone was waiting for the arrival of the new priest, but nobody came, except old Don Anselmo, who for years had had the parish of Torretta, two miles away. Since the two villages were so close, he had obviously been asked to fill in until a replacement was found for Don Camillo.

Don Anselmo looked around during his first Mass, and saw that there were only two people in the church, himself and his acolyte. And the acolyte was there only because Don

Anselmo had called for him at his own house. Things went on this way for some time, until Don Anselmo went to talk to the Bishop.

"Monsignore," he concluded, "that's not all. It's a serious business. They are acting as if neither church nor priest were there. No one comes to confession. 'I'll go when Don Camillo returns,' they are saying. When babies are born, they don't bring them to be baptized. 'That can wait for Don Camillo,' is their refrain. And they get married in the town hall and say they'll wait for Don Camillo to perform a church wedding. So far no one has died, and I suppose there'll be no necessity for a funeral until Don Camillo comes to conduct it."

The Bishop threw out his arms in despair.

"That blesséd Don Camillo is fated to be a thorn in my flesh even when he's not there!" he sighed. "But people must get it into their heads that he made a mistake and has to pay for it."

Don Anselmo shrugged his shoulders.

"It is my duty to report on everything I know," he said. "And I may as well tell you that many people don't think it was a mistake for Don Camillo to snatch the pitchfork away from someone who was trying to stick it into his stomach."

"Quite right," the Bishop agreed. "It wasn't a mistake to snatch it away; the mistake was to hit those two fellows over the head with the handle."

"Even then, some people think that Don Camillo had right on his side," Don Anselmo said in a respectful manner. "It is my further duty to inform you that under the circumstances I should have done the same thing myself."

The Bishop raised his eyes to Heaven.

"Lord, forgive this old madman!" he exclaimed. "He doesn't know what he is saying."

Don Anselmo was not just an impulsive boy; he was well on toward eighty, and now he hung his head in embarrassment, but continued to be of the same opinion. The Bishop delivered a long and very wise sermon, and ended up by saying: "Now go on house-to-house visits, to explain to the people that Don Camillo made a mistake and must be punished for it. It's up to you to make them see reason."

Don Anselmo went from house to house, and everywhere he received the same answer.

"If he did make a mistake, then it's only right that he should pay. We're waiting for him to finish paying and come back, that's all."

Meanwhile the Reds were beside themselves with joy. They had got Don Camillo out of the way, and no one was going to church. One evening Peppone accosted Don Anselmo.

"It's sad to see an old racket like the Vatican closing down," he sighed. "If we weren't excommunicated, we'd come to your Mass ourselves! Anyhow, if you decide to rent the premises, give me an option on them."

Don Anselmo did not let himself be perturbed.

"I can't even ask you to rent me your brain in return!" he retorted. "You rented that out a long time ago. I only hope you didn't let your soul go with it."

Then it began to rain. It rained on the mountains and in the valleys. Old oak trees were shattered by lightning, the sea foamed up in a storm, the rivers began to swell, and as the rain continued, they overflowed their banks and flooded whole towns with their muddy waters. Most dangerous of all, the mighty Po was rising, pressing harder and harder against its embankments. During the war, the embankment was bombed at a point called La Pioppa, and they had got around to mending it only within the last two years. Everyone looked fearfully at La Pioppa, feeling sure that if the pressure became too great, this was the point where the embankment would give way. The earth hadn't had time to pack solidly, and whereas the rest of the bank would hold, just as it had always held before, La Pioppa would crumble.

Meanwhile it continued to rain, night and day, and after each momentary respite, it came down harder than before. The papers were filled with news of squalls, floods, and landslides, but the village people thought only of their own danger. Already a lot of old crones were saying:

"Ever since Don Camillo went away, taking the altar crucifix with him, there's been trouble brewing."

The crucifix had a long-standing association with the river. Every year the people of the village carried it in a procession to the banks where the priest gave the waters his blessing. The old crones shook their heads.

"As long as he was here, we were protected. But now he's gone away."

As the river rose, they spoke more and more of the crucifix, and even the wisest among them lost their heads. One morning the Bishop found a village delegation waiting upon him.

"Give us back our crucifix," they implored. "We must form a procession right away and hold a blessing of the waters. Otherwise the village will be swept away."

The Bishop sighed.

"Brethen, have you so little faith?" he asked them. "God seems to be not within your souls but extraneous to them, if you pin all your trust in a wooden image, and without its help fall into despair."

Some of the men of the delegation hung their heads. And one of them, old Bonesti, stepped forward to say:

"We have faith in God, but we have lost faith in ourselves. All of us love our country, but when we go into battle, we need to see our regimental flag. The flag keeps us fighting for the country whose love is within us. That crucifix was our flag, and Don Camillo our flag-bearer. If we can have our flag back, we will face our troubles more courageously."

Don Camillo came back during the night, when no one was expecting him. But he had no sooner walked from the rectory to the church the next morning than the whole village knew it. They crowded to hear his first Mass, and afterwards they gathered around him to say:

"We want a procession!"

"Christ has gone back to His altar, and there He stays," said Don Camillo severely. "He'll not move until we hold the regular procession next year. This year, the waters have been blessed already."

"Yes, but the river is rising."

"He knows that," said Don Camillo. "No one needs to refresh His memory. All I can do is pray that Christ give us strength to bear our sufferings serenely."

The people were obsessed with fear, and when they insisted on a procession, Don Camillo had to speak to them even more sternly than before.

"Have a procession, then, but rather than carry a wooden cross about the streets, carry Christ in your hearts! Let every one of you hold a private procession of this kind. Have faith in God, and not in graven images. And then God will help you."

But the people's fear continued to rise, along with the river. Engineers came to inspect La Pioppa and declared it would hold, but they advised the villagers to get their belongings together and be prepared for evacuation. The engineers went away at ten o'clock in the morning, and at eleven the water was still rising. Then fear turned into terror.

"There's no time to save anything," someone was saying. "The only thing to do is to cross the river and cut an opening in the embankment on the other side."

:[226]:

No one knew who was the first person to suggest this blasphemy, but very soon everyone was repeating it. Eighty people out of a hundred were trying to figure out the best way to cross the river and make a cut that would channel the overflow to the opposite shore. Sooner or later someone might have actually done it. But all of a sudden the rain ceased, and hope returned to their hearts. The church bells called them to the square, and there Don Camillo addressed them.

"There's only one thing to do, and that is to carry our most important belongings to safety."

Just then the rain began to fall again.

"There's no time!" the people shouted. "La Pioppa won't hold."

"Yes, it will," said Don Camillo firmly.

"That's what you say!" they shouted.

"That's the word left by the engineers," said Don Camillo.

"It's only a word!" someone shouted.

"It's a fact, I say!" Don Camillo retorted. "I'm so sure it will hold that I'll go stand on the weakest point of the embankment. If I'm mistaken, then I'll pay!"

Don Camillo raised his big umbrella and walked toward the river, with a crowd following after him. They followed him along the embankment until he came to the newly-built stretch at La Pioppa. There Don Camillo turned around.

"Let everyone go pack up his things calmly," he called out. "I'll wait at La Pioppa for you to finish."

He walked on, and fifty yards farther he came to the exact point where everyone thought there would be a break. The crowd looked in bewilderment first at the priest and then at the raging water.

"I'm coming to keep you company," a voice shouted, and out of the crowd stepped Peppone, with all eyes upon him.

"The embankment will hold," Peppone shouted; "there's

:[227]:

no danger. Don't do anything silly, but prepare to evacuate in good order, under the chief councilman's direction. To prove my confidence in the embankment, I'll stay right here."

When they saw the priest and the mayor at the point of what they thought was the greatest danger, the people hurried to get their livestock out of the stables and load their household goods on trucks and wagons. The rain continued to come down and the river to rise, and the village population made ready. Meanwhile Don Camillo and Peppone sat on two big stones under the umbrella.

"You'd be better off if you were still exiled in the mountains, Father," said Peppone.

"Oh, I don't know about that," Don Camillo answered.

Peppone was silent for a few minutes and then clapped his hand to his hip.

"If this thing were to break while people are still loading their things and we're sitting here, that would be a pretty mess! We'd be done for and so would they."

"It would be a great deal worse if we'd saved ourselves by cutting the embankment dealing out death and destruction on the other side. You must admit there's a difference between misfortune and crime."

Peppone shrugged his shoulders.

"I've got the better of you, in any case."

Toward evening the rain paused and the river fell. The village had been completely evacuated, and Don Camillo and Peppone left the embankment and went home. As they crossed the church square, Don Camillo said:

"You might thank God for saving your skin. You owe that good luck to Him."

"True enough," said Peppone. "But He saved your skin too, and that's enough bad luck to make us even!"

THE RIGHT BELL

THE RIVER EMBANKMENT
did not give way, even where everyone said it was sure to
crack, and so the next morning many people went back to the
village, which lay below the water-level, in order to fetch more
of their belongings. But toward nine o'clock something unexpected happened. The water had risen higher and although it
did not penetrate the main embankment, it found a weak spot
elsewhere.

About a mile east of the village, the road running along the
embankment went over a bridge across the Fossone, a tribu-

tary which poured at this point into the Po. The Fossone had solid banks of its own, but because the Po was so high, it had reversed its course and was running away from instead of into the river. Just below the bridge, where the banks of the Fossone joined those of the river, the water tunnelled underneath and then came up in a jet, making the hole larger and larger. There was no way of holding it, and the villagers soon returned with wagons and trucks to seek safety.

Don Camillo had worked all alone until three o'clock in the morning, carrying things to the second floor and attic of the rectory. Then he was so tired that he fell into a dead sleep. At half-past nine in the morning he was awakened by the shouts of people running to take refuge on the embankment. Soon the noise died away, and he got up to look out of the window at the deserted church square. He went down to explore further and then climbed up in the bell tower. From this vantage point he could see that the water had already crept up on the lower part of the village and was slowly creeping higher. It had encircled the isolated hut of old Merola, and when it reached the ground-floor windows the whole thing crumbled. Don Camillo sighed. The old man had not wanted to leave, and it was by sheer force that they had taken him away. Now the pace of the advancing water was faster; the rain had left the earth so thoroughly soaked that it could not absorb a drop. It was up to the higher part of the village, which lay stretched out perfectly flat before it. Hearing a crash in the distance, he looked through his field-glasses and saw that a hundred and fifty feet of one bank of the Fossone had given away. Then, going over to another window, he noticed a crowd of people on the main embankment gazing in the direction of the village.

Those who had gone with their trucks and wagons for a second load of their belongings had been forced back. Now they stood with evacuees from other villages, who had brought their livestock and household goods with them, looking down at the newly flooded area, half a mile away. No one spoke, and old women shed silent tears. Their village seemed to be dying there before them, and they began to think of it as already dead.

"There is no God!" said an old man gloomily.

But just as that moment the church bell rang. There was no mistaking the sound, even if the tone was somewhat different from usual. All eyes were fixed on the church tower.

After Don Camillo had seen the crowd on the embankment he went back to the ground. The water had climbed the three steps leading to the church door and was running into the nave.

"Lord, forgive me for forgetting that it is Sunday," said Don Camillo, kneeling in front of the altar.

Before going to prepare himself in the sacristy, Don Camillo stepped into the little room at the base of the bell tower, whose floor was lower than that of the church and already covered with eight or ten inches of water. He tugged at a rope, hoping that it was the right one. It was, and when the crowd on the embankment heard it ring, they said:

"Eleven o'clock Mass!"

The women joined their hands in prayer and the men took off their hats.

Don Camillo lit the candles and began to say Mass. The water was climbing the altar steps and soon it touched his vestments. It was muddy and cold, but Don Camillo paid no attention. His congregation was dry and safe on the embankment. And when it was time for the sermon, he did not mind the fact that the church was empty, but preached to his parishioners just as if they were there before him. There were three feet of water in the nave, and pews and confessionals had overturned and were floating at random. The door was wide open, and beyond it he could see the submerged houses on the square and the lowering clouds on the horizon.

"Brethren," he said, "the waters have boiled up from the river bed and now are sweeping everything before them. But one day they will be calmed and return to their rightful place and the sun will shine again. Even if you lose everything you have, you can still be rich in your faith in God. Only those who doubt God's mercy and justice will be impoverished, even if their possessions are intact."

And he went on at considerable length in the flooded church, while from the embankment people continued to stare at the tower. When the bell sounded for the elevation, the women knelt down on the damp ground and the men bowed their heads. Then the bell rang again for the final blessing. The Mass was over, and people moved about freely and talked in a low tone of voice, hoping to hear the bell again. Soon afterward it rang out gaily once more, and the men took out their watches and said:

"Noon! It's time to go for dinner."

They got into whatever vehicles they had with them and went to the improvised canteens and shelters. And looking back over their shoulders at the village, which seemed to be afloat in a sea of mud, they were obviously thinking:

"As long as Don Camillo's there, everything's all right."

Before Don Camillo went back to the rectory he looked up at Christ above the altar.

"Forgive me, Lord, for not kneeling. If I were to kneel, I'd be in water up to the neck."

His head was bent and he could not be sure that Christ had smiled. But he was almost sure that He had, for there was a glow in his heart that made him forget the fact that he was

:[232]:

soaked to the waist. He was able to get to the rectory, seizing on the way a floating ladder, with which he managed to climb into a second-storey window. He changed his clothes, had something to eat and went to bed. Toward three in the afternoon there was a knock at the window.

"Come in," said Don Camillo, and there was Peppone.

"If you'll come down, there's a boat rowed by some of my boys waiting for you," Peppone mumbled.

When a man is lying in bed, or even sitting up in it, he is in no position to come out with a phrase that will go down in history. So Don Camillo leaped to his feet and shouted:

"The old guard dies, but it never surrenders!"

Although he was on his feet, he had nothing on but his drawers, and this detracted from the solemnity of the occasion. But Peppone was in no mood to notice.

"Then devil take you," he said angrily. "You may not get another chance to escape so soon!"

The rescue squad rowed on. When the boat passed in front of the open church door, Peppone shouted to the rowers to watch out on the left. While they were looking in the other direction, he had time to take off his cap and put it back on without being observed. For the rest of the way he cudgelled his brain to know what Don Camillo had meant about the old guard that dies but never surrenders. Even if the water stood eight feet high, the flood seemed to him to have abated since he knew that Don Camillo was at his post.

Maroli was as old as sin, and all skin and bones, but at times he could be as hard-headed as a young man of twenty-five. When the flood became really serious, his two sons loaded all their belongings onto wagons and prepared to take their families away, but the old man refused to budge. He said as much to his daughters-in-law when they came to carry him down from the bed to which he had been invalided for some time. And the two women told their husbands to do something about it themselves, because there was no use arguing with a madman. The sons and two grandsons went upstairs to try to persuade him, but they received the same answer.

"Here is my home, and here I stay."

His sons explained that the whole village was being evácuated because at any moment the river might overflow its banks, but Maroli only shook his head.

"I'm a sick man and I can't stand the exposure. I'm staying here."

The daughters-in-law came up again to tell their husbands to hurry. And one of them said:

"Don't be silly. No sick people are being left outside in the bad weather. They're all sheltered and taken care of."

Maroli sat up in bed and pointed a rheumatic finger at her.

"I see now. You want to get me away from here and into an institution. For a long time you've been looking for a way to get rid of me. But I don't want to go to the hospital and die there, alone, like a dog. I'll die here, among my own things, even if I am in your way. Here, in this bed where my wife died, I intend to breathe my last. And you must bury me beside her."

All of them together tried to persuade him, but he held fast. Finally his older son came close to the bed.

"That's enough talking," he shouted. "You take his other shoulder, and you two women hold his feet. We'll carry him down on the mattress."

"Go away, the lot of you," the old man protested.

But they were all around him, holding onto the mattress. A minute more, and they would have lifted it up without the least difficulty, because the old man was light as a feather. He took hold of the shirt-front of his older son and tried to push him away, but the son was beside himself with exasperation and tore himself loose. He threw the old man back on the bed and held him down.

:[235]:

"Stop this crazy stuff, or I'll bash your head in!" he shouted.

The old man tried to free himself, but it was as if a stone were bearing down on his chest and he could do nothing but suffer.

"Rosa! . . . Rosa! . . ." he called.

But what was a twelve-year-old girl to do?

She threw herself like an angry cat at the man who was pinning him to the bed, but a dozen hands caught hold of her, pushed her aside and slapped her.

"Keep out of this, you stupid girl! Are you crazy?"

The old man was breathless with rage.

"*You're* crazy!" he shouted. "And chicken-hearted too! If her father were alive, you wouldn't dare treat me this way."

But Rosa's father was dead and buried, and so was her mother. The father was Maroli's favorite and most promising son, and his death had broken the old man's heart.

"We're all you've got now," said his oldest, jeeringly, "and you'll have to do what we say. Let's hurry."

A dozen impatient arms raised up the mattress, while the heavy hands of the oldest son kept the old man still. Just then they heard Rosa's voice:

"Let go of him, or I'll shoot!"

A shotgun in the hands of a young girl is more terrifying than a Tommy gun in those of a man. And Rosa was not only a young girl, but not quite right in the head as well, so that naturally enough the owners of the dozen hands (two men, two women and two boys) agreed to let the old man go. They put down the mattress and the oldest son withdrew his hands.

"Go away, or I'll fire!" said the girl.

They backed out of the door and when they were gone the girl chained it.

"I'll send the police and a male nurse after you," shouted the oldest son from the stairs.

:[236]:

The old man was undaunted.

"Better mind your own business, because if anyone comes near I'll burn the house down," he retorted.

As in all the peasant houses of the region, there was a direct connection between the living quarters and the stable. The old man's room was just above this, and next door to the hayloft. He had chosen this room, formerly used to store wheat, because he could look through a hole in the floor and see the animals in the stable below as well as the movements of the men who took care of them. The hayloft was full of hay, and with a piece of tow on the end of a stick he could very easily set it on fire. For this reason his threat threw the rest of the family into a cold perspiration. The old man had a shotgun, a kerosene lamp, a can of kerosene and a mad girl at his disposal.

"We'll leave you alone," they called back from the stair.

"You'd better!" he said mockingly.

When they got out into the yard one of the daughters-in-law had a bright idea and called up to the old man's window:

"If you choose to stay, that's your own business. But let the girl go. You have no right to expose her to danger. Let her come along with us."

The old man was momentarily taken aback.

"Rosa," he said, "the water's rising and there may be danger. If you want to be safe, go along."

The girl shook her head and closed the shutters.

"God blast the two of them!" said the bright daughter-in-law.

And the grandsons observed that if both the old man and the girl were to perish, it would be a gain to everybody, themselves included. Maroli's two sons maintained a gloomy silence. But when they and their possessions had reached safety they looked in the direction of the house and the older one said angrily:

:[237]:

"This won't last forever. And when we go back, we'll have to put things in order. He must be sent to a hospital and she to an asylum."

"Yes," said his brother approvingly. "They can't get away with it any longer."

The old man and the girl remained alone in the house and no one knew that they were there. When she was sure that the last of the family had gone, she went downstairs, locked the doors and bolted the windows. There was plenty to eat in the kitchen and the old man told her what to bring upstairs. Finally he had her put an empty barrel in his room and gradually fill it with buckets of water from the pump below. When evening came she was dead tired and lay down on a mattress on the floor.

"That blessed family may come back," the old man grumbled. "You go ahead and sleep and I'll watch out for them. If I hear anything I'll call you."

He sat on the edge of his bed, shotgun in hand, but nobody came. The next morning the river overflowed its banks and the water rose to within two feet of the downstairs ceiling.

"Now we can set our minds at rest," said the old man.

Toward eleven o'clock they heard a bell ringing and the old man sent the girl to look out the attic window. She came down after some time and said:

"The church door is open and there's water everywhere. And there's a crowd of people up on the embankment."

At three o'clock she went up to look again and ran down to report:

"There's a boat going around from one house to another."

"Rosa, if you want to go, go," the old man sighed.

"If they come for us we'll set fire to the hayloft," she answered.

:[238]:

The boat came through their yard, and the girl looked out at it through a crack in the shutters.

"There's that big mechanic who always wears a red kerchief," she said to the old man.

And a minute later Peppone called out:

"Is there anyone here?"

The old man and the girl held their breath, and the boat went away.

"The family must have been scared to say anything about us," muttered the old man. "Now we can have some peace and quiet."

Don Camillo awakened suddenly and found himself in the dark. He was so tired that he had fallen asleep in the afternoon, and now evening had overtaken him. When he threw open the window he looked out over an expanse of water as wide as the sea, and saw on the horizon a red fringe left by the sunset. The silence was oppressive, and the memory of cheerfully lighted houses seemed very far away. Now the houses were all blacked out and the water came to within two feet of the ground-floor ceilings. The distant howl of a dog reminded him of his own Thunder. Where was Thunder now? Where had the flood surprised him? The howling continued, and now it seemed to come from directly below and filled him with a mixture of anxiety and fear. He lit the lamp, took a piece of iron and pried up a piece of the floor. There was Thunder, floating on a raft. And the raft was the downstairs table.

Thunder must have been caught by the flood away from home, and God only knows how he had been saved. When the first wave had subsided he must have swum back and in through the front door. Here he would have been a prisoner had not the table left downstairs by Don Camillo provided him with a perch and safety. The water had stopped rising and

:[239]:

Thunder waited for help from above, until help actually did come from the ceiling. Don Camillo pulled him through the hole, and Thunder shook himself so joyfully that his master was splashed all over.

It was time to ring the Ava Maria bell. Don Camillo was of the school which believes that the old guard dies but never surrenders, and as a corollary to this he believed that the old guard should not resort to swimming for transportation. With four empty gasoline cans and a big washing-board he had built himself a raft, upon which he now made his way to the church to talk on his knees to Christ on the Cross above the submerged altar.

"Lord, forgive me for bringing Thunder to Your house, but he is the only living creature in the village and I couldn't leave him behind. As a matter of fact, You've seen many a church-goer that's more of a dog than Thunder . . . And forgive me for attaching my old army field altar to the bell tower and saying Mass over there. A flood is something like a war, and I feel as if I had been called to combat duty."

Christ sighed.

"Don Camillo, what are you doing here?" He asked. "Shouldn't you be with your people?"

"My people are here," Don Camillo answered. "Their bodies may be far away, but they are here in their hearts."

"But, Don Camillo, your strong arms are inactive and useless, instead of bringing help to those who are weaker than yourself."

"I can best help them by ringing the familiar bell to keep up their hope and faith while they are gone. And then, Lord, when Thunder was lost he came to look for me at home rather than among the evacuees. Which means that my post is here."

"It's a pretty poor fellow that looks to an animal for a rule of conduct rather than to his own powers of reason. God gave you a brain to think with, not a dog."

"But God gave me a heart, too. The heart may not reason, but sometimes it is more powerful than the brain. Forgive my heart and Thunder . . ."

Don Camillo tied up the raft below his bedroom window and went to sleep. Because of the oppressive silence, he slept for a very long time. He was awakened by the barking of Thunder who was jumping up at the window. Don Camillo took his shotgun and without lighting the lamp peered out between the closed shutters. Someone called him, and he played his flashlight over the water below. He saw a big vat with a bundle of rags stirring at the bottom.

"Who's there?" he called.

"Rosa Maroli," said the bundle of rags. "Grandfather wants to see you."

"Grandfather?"

"He's sick, and wants to die like a Christian."

Don Camillo put the girl on his raft and pushed off with a long pole in his hand.

"What in Heaven's name are you doing here?" he asked her.

"Grandfather wanted to stay and I want to keep him company."

"Haven't you been scared?"

"No, grandfather was there. And we could see a light in the rectory and hear the church bell."

Old Maroli had not much longer to live.

"They wanted to send me to the hospital to die like a dog," he said. "But I want to die a Christian death in my own house . . . And they said I was crazy . . . yes, and that she was crazy too."

The girl stared at him dumbly.

"Rosa," he panted, "is it true that you're crazy?"

:[241]:

She shook her head.

"Sometimes my head aches and I can't seem to understand," she said timidly.

"Her head aches, do you hear?" said the old man. "She fell on a stone when she was little, and there's a bone pressing on her brain. The doctor told me that himself. He told me they could fix her up with an operation. Then I took ill, and the others wouldn't spend the money . . . They want to send her to the asylum, because it hurts their consciences to see her around."

"Calm yourself; I'm here," said Don Camillo, trying to check the old man's growing excitement.

"You must arrange for that operation . . ." said the old man. "Now, just pull my bed out a little. . . . There on the wall . . . Lift out that striped brick . . ."

Don Camillo moved the brick and found a heavy bag behind it.

"Gold!" panted the old man. "Gold coins . . . All mine, and all for her! Have her operated, and send her to stay with someone who can give her an education. We'll show them how crazy we are, Rosa, won't we?"

The girl nodded.

"I want to die like a Christian," panted the old man.

When Don Camillo rose from his knees, it was dawn. Old man Maroli had died like a Christian, and the girl was staring with wide-open eyes at his motionless body.

"Come with me," said Don Camillo gently. "No one will upset your grandfather any more. And no one will upset you, either."

He took hold of a chair and with his enormous hands broke a leg in two as easily as if it were a breadstick.

"That's what I'll do to anyone who touches you."

Thunder waited for them, barking, at Don Camillo's window. The priest poled up to it and told the girl to go through.

"Lie down on the first bed you find," he said, "and have a good sleep."

Then he went over to the church and stopped in front of the altar.

"Lord," he said, "now you see what I meant. She said herself that she wasn't afraid because she could see my light and hear the church bell ring . . . And she isn't crazy. She had a bad fall as a child. The operation will cure that."

"You must have had a bad fall as a child, too," said Christ with a smile. "But there's nothing can cure you. You'll always listen to your heart rather than your brain . . . may God keep that heart of yours whole!"

Thunder kept watch at the foot of the bed where Rosa lay sleeping. The bell tolled for old man Maroli's death, but no one heard it, because the wind carried the sound away.

APPOINTMENT AT MIDNIGHT

AT LAST THE BIG RIVER
returned to its bed and the people were busy putting their
land and homes in order. A thick autumn fog hung over the
drenched valley but everyone felt the danger had passed and
that above the mist, the sky was serene. And so, in fact, it was;
but just as surely as the waters receded and the threat of the
flood passed so did trouble of another kind flare up in the
village.

It had all begun one day in July, when Peppone and his
gang appeared in full force at the rectory.

"We want a *Te Deum!*" Peppone shouted. "A public thanksgiving. Someone has shot at our national Leader."

Don Camillo was perplexed.

"I understand," he said calmly, "but I don't see why we should hold a service of thanksgiving just because a poor devil has been shot. Say what you like, he's a human being."

Peppone clenched his fists.

"We want to give thanks because he wasn't killed! And don't try to be funny, because we're in a state of national emergency. So here's the plan. You organize the *Te Deum*, complete with music, singing, flowers, curtains, lighting effects, and bells, and announce it by means of a poster with an angel on either side on the church door. Meanwhile we'll print leaflets and put them prominently on display. Then we'll see who shows up. Everyone that fails to show up is a filthy reactionary. We'll take down the names of the absent and then make a series of house-to-house visits."

"Well spoken, Chief," Smilzo said solemnly. "We must first indentify and then punish all those guilty of incitement to public disorder. The people have had quite enough!"

Don Camillo looked over at him.

"Are you going to list the names?" he asked.

"Of course," said Smilzo.

"Then put mine down at the head of the list, because I won't be at the thanksgiving service."

Peppone pushed his hat back on his head and put his hands on his hips.

"So you refuse to publicly thank the Almighty for having saved an honest man from an attempted crime, is that it?"

"No. I won't let a religious service give you and your hotheads an excuse to beat up innocent people. If you really want to thank the Almighty, come with your friends and I'll say a Mass, just as I did yesterday when Gigino Forcella fell off the roof without getting a single scratch on his body."

:[245]:

Peppone brought his fist down on the table.

"The people want a solemn ceremony, a *Te Deum,* I tell you, not just an everyday Mass. This is a cause for national thanksgiving."

"The thanksgiving is a strictly private affair," Don Camillo insisted. "Every good Christian should rejoice when his neighbor is saved from danger, to be sure. But by your reasoning Gigino Forcella's family was entitled to a *Te Deum* too."

Peppone's face looked like an advertisement for apoplexy.

"How can you mention Gigino Forcella in the same breath with our Leader? Gigino doesn't interest anyone outside his own family anyhow. And our Leader is known the world over."

Don Camillo was not impressed.

"Gigino Forcella's family is a small one, while that of your Leader is made up of several million people. That's the only difference. It's a bigger family, if you like, but it doesn't include the whole nation. If the local members of your Leader's family want me to say a special Mass, I'll be glad to oblige them. But in view of the threats you made a few minutes ago it will have to be a purely family affair. I won't have anyone that doesn't belong to your Party in the church. Otherwise I should be abetting your blackmail. People must come to church of their own free will and not because of the fear of punshment. The church is no place for political propaganda."

Smilzo pulled the visor of his cap around to one side, put his hands on his hips and looked up at Don Camillo.

"Look who's talking!" he said with a leer. "If there happened to be a God, He'd freeze you to the ground for such a shameless lie."

As for Peppone, he was bursting with things to say but didn't know where to begin.

"You Judas!" he shouted. "You've sold Christ for thirty American dollars!"

"Don't pay him any attention, Chief," Smilzo begged him. "Certain people can't be treated any other way."

He took a notebook out of his pocket, licked the point of his pencil and wrote something down.

"Don Camillo!" he said. "Exclamation point! Now that you're on my blacklist not even the Almighty can save you!"

And Peppone added:

"Keep your *Te Deums* and your Masses as well. The Party has no use for your Madonna and saints. And here's what I'll do to the next Party member that sets foot in your church!"

So saying, he picked up a chair and crushed the backboard of it in his fingers, looking straight into Don Camillo's eyes.

"Mind you get it mended now," Don Camillo said calmly.

Peppone made no answer, but turned on his heels, and walked out, followed by his gang, who slammed the door behind them. A moment later Smilzo came back, with a defiant look on his face, picked up the chair and bore it away. He held his head high and his chest stuck out, and he strutted as triumphantly as if he represented the inevitable onward march of the proletarian revolution.

Don Camillo got his chair back but Peppone and Peppone's followers and their families stayed away from church.

Three months later Bigio had a baby, but as he was a Party member the question of a baptism never came up. When Bigio saw the priest coming he dodged out of the way, but one evening Don Camillo managed to stop him.

"If it's in obedience to Party orders that you're not coming to church, *transeat*, I can let that go by. Your sins are on your own conscience. But you let your son come at least once in his life, to be baptized. Or have you already enrolled him in the Party?"

Bigio, who was the most reasonable of the gang, threw out his arms.

"The order goes for the whole family," he said. "If the Chief were to know that I'd had my baby baptized he'd take my hide off."

"Peppone doesn't have to know," Don Camillo suggested.

That night they brought the baby to him for a clandestine baptism. That was all Don Camillo managed to achieve, but he was not discouraged.

"Lord," he said to Christ, at the altar, "I'm waiting for Christmas. In all the years that I've been here they've never missed the midnight Mass. A few years ago, when Giubai was wanted by the police, he came on Christmas Eve and I saw him in the far corner, with his coat collar turned up all around his face. Lord, just have confidence in me!"

"I've always had confidence in you," Christ said to him with a smile, "but can you have confidence in yourself?"

"Well . . . to a certain extent. I have more faith in You."

As Christmas approached Don Camillo tried to find out which way the wind was blowing, and word came back to him that husbands and wives were arguing over the question, with the wives maintaining that on Christmas Eve they really must break the rule. As the time grew shorter and shorter, the arguments became more and more heated, until finally the women flatly declared: "We and the children are going to church; you can do what you please." Peppone, whose wife had given him an unforgettable kick in the shins, was well aware of what was brewing and finally decided to leave the women and children free while the men kept up the boycott. They had said they wouldn't set foot in the church, and they would stick to their word. In order to prevent any last-minute weakening Peppone summoned the men to an appointment in the People's Palace. There they would answer the challenge of the Midnight Mass with a democratic "midnight cell meeting," whose ceremonial would consist of readings from the classics of the religion of Marx and Lenin and selected passages from such great democrats as Stalin and his ilk.

When Christmas Eve came the church was filled with candlelight and singing, while on the hard benches of the bare People's Palace the men listened to Peppone reading things none of them understood. Every now and then the wind blew a few notes from the church organ against the closed windows. The Mass was over early, because something was tormenting Don Camillo's mind. When he was left alone in the church he took off his vestments and padlocked the church door. He walked up and down for several minutes and then stopped before Christ on the Cross.

"Lord," he said, "Did You see?"

"Yes, I saw," Christ answered. "You were over-confident. You relied too much on your own powers."

"No, that isn't it," said Don Camillo. "I pinned all my faith on You."

"And so now you've lost your faith, is that it then?"

"Never!" said Don Camillo indignantly. "If a starving man sees a crust of bread on the table before him, he can't just sit tight and say: 'I knew God wouldn't let me die of hunger.' God isn't going to put it in his mouth; he must stretch out his hand. To have faith that God will provide doesn't dispense a fellow from using his head. If the bread doesn't jump into his mouth, he has to go get it. The Scriptures tell us that if the mountain doesn't go to Christ, then Christ will go to the mountain."

Christ smiled.

"Only it's not me, it's Mohammed," he objected.

"Forgive me," said the chagrined Don Camillo. "I only meant . . ."

"There's nothing to forgive, Don Camillo. It's not words that count, it's intentions."

Don Camillo ran his big hand over his forehead and looked up at Christ. But he was thinking of Mohammed, and Christ knew it and smiled.

"Comrades," Peppone was saying, "as a fitting close to this meeting at which we have borne witness to our democratic faith, I shall read you a masterly profile of Mao Tse-Tung . . ."

Just then the door opened and in came a powerfully built man in a heavy coat, who made his way like a tank through the benches on which the men were sitting, went up onto the platform where Peppone was holding forth and set a gray-green box on the speaker's table. All the men in the front rows recognized the box immediately. They had seen it during the war, when Don Camillo risked German bullets in order to visit them up in the mountains. And automatically they rose to their feet. Don Camillo lifted the lid off the box, and there was his field altar. Peppone stepped quickly down from the platform, and a moment later, when Don Camillo turned around and grunted, Smilzo proudly leapt up beside him. As he had done so many times in the old days, he helped the priest don his vestments, lit the candles and knelt down at one side of the altar to serve him.

It was a simple Mass, military style, and of an almost clandestine character. But they had put out the lights in the hall, so that the candles on the little altar stood out in the dark. The organ notes that had blown against the closed windows were still vibrating and from the towers of church and town hall the chimes echoed through the valley while the golden wings of the great angel seemed to spread over the little world.